THE BEAUTY UNDERNEATH THE STRUGGLE

THE BEAUTY UNDERNEATH THE STRUGGLE

Creating Your BUS Story

By Niki Spears

© 2020 by Niki Spears

All rights reserved. This book or any portion thereof may not be reproduced or used in any manner whatsoever without the express written permission of the publisher except for the use of brief quotations in a book review.

ISBN: 9798646091506 (paperback)

LCCN: 2020909846

To my number one fan and biggest cheerleader, my husband, Kermit Spears; my amazing daughters, Bianca, Brandi, and Brooklynn; my granddaughter, Baelor; my son, Barry; and my loving and supportive parents, Lee and Mary Thomas. Thanks for loving me unconditionally.

Contents

Your Journey Starts Here!

Foreword xi

Preface..xiii

Introduction xv

1   BE Responsible- 100%...1

    A BUS Story 8

    You're Invited! 14

    Wake Up! Own 100 Percent of Your Story!.......16

    Uninvite Yourself from the Victim Party............18

    I Woke Up!...19

2   BE Aware..23

    Scroll all the way down!..24

    Follow the Why!..25

    Your Beliefs, Your Story..28

    Expanding Our Beliefs 30

    Every Experience, Every Thought Matters........31

    Your Beliefs Will Guide Your Why 34

Your Why...39

Identifying Your Writing Style.............................46

Their Story is not Your Story...............................50

3   BE Open..53

Overcoming Writer's Block...................................56

Limiting Beliefs..57

Negative Self-Talk...60

Fear of Failure/Unknown.....................................64

Clearing Past Blockages.......................................66

Editing Your Perceptions.....................................66

Leaning into Failure to Create Possibilities.........68

Time Is Unstoppable: Value It!.............................72

4   BE Courageous...79

Have Courage..79

Take Action...84

Casting Call: Positive Characters Wanted!...........86

Casting the Right People for the Right Roles........90

Focus on Something Bigger Than Yourself...........91

5   BE Grateful...99

The Power of Gratitude..99

So Give Thanks.. 102

Gratitude in Moments of Struggle..................... 109

Experience the *Joy* of Learning......................... 111

The Beauty Underneath the Struggle

Learning Doesn't Just Happen in the Classroom........113
Embracing New Beliefs..116
Your Legacy 118

6　BElieve..**123**
Your Story...123
Using the Eraser to Edit Your Story.........................126
Using Your Power of Choice to Write Your Story......128
The Choice Is Always Yours 130
Check Yourself Before You Wreck Yourself..............135
Love Your Story 137
Won't He Do It!...139
Struggles Need Love Too!..143

7　BE Awesome **145**
What Is Your Writing Style Now?.............................145
Owning Your Awesomeness 149

8　BE Free to BE YOU! Your BUS Story!............**155**

Workbook Exercises 159
Acknowledgments 177
Bibliography...179
Author Biography..181

ix

Foreword

I have never met a person like Shenique (Niki) Spears. Though she has given me credit for believing in her when she didn't believe in herself, I have always known her to be a woman of confidence and commitment. It is clear to me that early on she learned how to find the beauty underneath the struggle (BUS) to build a life that is based on setting and achieving goals.

At a recent high school graduation, the valedictorian admonished her peers, "Don't be embarrassed of your past self. Be proud that you've made it this far. Be proud that you have been able to change so much. Carry those lessons with you, and share them with others, all while you work to make your future self proud." In essence, this wise young person was asking her peers to develop their own BUS story. I was inspired to hear such wisdom from this young person.

It takes courage to do the work required to overcome the challenges of life, and we must be even more intentional about finding the beauty in that struggle. In his book, *Reboot*, Jerry Colonna writes, "Better humans make better leaders." I feel blessed that God has enabled me to overcome a childhood filled with trauma, loss, and abandonment. I am even more thankful that he has revealed to me the depth and value of the strength of character, positive personality traits, and capacity for leadership I developed because of those struggles—the beauty underneath. Niki is inviting us on this journey of self-exploration. Each of us facing our own unique challenges to exert ownership of our thoughts, feelings, and behaviors to claim the empowered life we dream about and to be the leader we are called to be.

Niki is more than an educator, speaker, and author. She is a wife, mother, Lolly, and friend. During our fourteen-year friendship, I have watched her inspire and empower others to achieve higher levels of success and leadership. Niki has left her mark each step of her journey, and I am proud that she is now sharing her own story with the world and challenging readers to create their own BUS story.

I am privileged to introduce you to my friend, Niki Spears.

Charles E. Dupre, Ed.D.
June 2020

Preface

For several years, I've been encouraged by close family members and friends to write a book. My life, much like yours, has been riddled with good times, hardships, celebrations, and struggles. These webs of experiences have been difficult for me to untangle as I try to determine where to start and what part of my story to share with the public.

After countless learning experiences, I have finally settled on my first message to share. I have been inspired by so many of my readings on my life journey by spiritual teachers like Deepak Chopra, Wayne Dyer, Erckhart Tolle, Don Miguel Ruiz, and many more who have helped me redefine painful moments in my life as moments of growth and renewal.

While reading Bobby Herrera's *The Gift of Struggle*, I was drawn to chapter one as he shares one moment that changed his life.

Mr. Herrera gives his account of a moment that happened when he was seventeen years old and he and his brother played on a basketball team that had just won a game. After the game, the coach took the team to dinner at a local restaurant. All the basketball players except for Bobby and his brother exited the bus. They stayed behind because they didn't have money to pay for a meal. Surprisingly, the father of one of his teammates reboarded the bus and said, "It would make me very happy if you would allow me to buy you boys dinner so you can join the rest of the team. No one else has to know. To thank me, you just have to do the same thing in the future for another great kid like yourself." Mr. Herrera says he'll never forget the gratitude he felt at this moment and how this simple act of kindness had a profound impact on his life. He calls this moment on the bus his bus story.

After reading Mr. Herrera's story and reflecting on my own, I believe we all have a bus story, several bus stories to be exact. A story about finding *the beauty underneath the struggle*. When I look back at every challenge or struggle in my life, there was always a unique lesson to learn that would further propel me forward on my journey, teaching me new things about myself and the world around me.

This is why I am excited to bring to you my first book, titled *The Beauty underneath the Struggle: Creating Your BUS Story*.

Introduction

" Are you ready to create the life of your dreams?
Ready to morph into a better version of yourself and take
charge of your story? "

The word *struggle* can carry discouraging thoughts of conflict, controversy, tension, and opposition. The struggle
between where we are now and where we wish to be has
stirred in the minds of human beings for as long as anyone
can remember. We live with the belief that without struggle,
there is eternal bliss. This is not true. It is because of struggle
that bliss exists. Struggle introduces us to a purposeful life,
and once we understand the treasures it holds, we will then
be able to see the opportunity in every challenge.

When we are faced with challenging situations, we tend
to do one of two things—resist the experience altogether
(fight) or adopt a belief that somehow, we are being tar-
geted, which will result in a victim mindset (suffer). Either of
these behaviors can lead to a domino effect of creating even
more suffering because the more we push something away,

the stronger it becomes. True strength is in allowing yourself to feel sad, anxious, or scared. You see, emotions are neither good nor bad, unless we get stuck in one for too long or react in ways that will lead to more unfortunate outcomes. For example, anger can be helpful when it gives you energy to take a stand for something you believe in, and it can be harmful if it encourages you to do or say things that hurt people. This book is my invitation for you to join me on a journey of writing your special BUS story. It is for those who are ready to find the *beauty underneath the struggle.*

This journey is not for the faint of heart; it is for those who have the courage to expand their life story. It is for those who will allow struggle to become their teacher or guide to a new world with tremendous possibilities. Once we stop seeing struggle as the enemy of our desires and start seeing it as a partner, we will no longer hold on to the pain of trying to reject or block something that will help to mold us into what we are meant to be. So prepare to embrace struggle in a new way, so you can begin to see the hidden opportunities that lie beneath.

As I write, we are in the midst of the COVID-19 pandemic, caused by the coronavirus, which has been impacting people from all over the world for some time. Thousands of people in the United States and around the world have lost their lives, and many of us are confined to our homes, unable to participate in events or functions as we did before. It's moments like these that make us feel like the universe is grabbing us by the shoulders and giving us a good shake, trying to wake us up from our current state of mind so that we rise to a level of courage and feel empowered to do the work we were created to do. It's in these moments that we are reminded we are only on this earth for a brief period of time, and we must stop taking this life for granted and start living now! It's in these times that we begin to reflect on our own lives and what it means. Creating a BUS story is being brave enough to embrace our struggles. This pandemic will undoubtedly be included in our history books as an important time in our world for generations to come. What will this moment say about you? Will you become a victim of these circumstances, or will you join me and find the beauty underneath the struggle and create your best BUS story?

Before advancing to the next page, let's make sure you are prepared for the journey on which you are about to embark so that by the end of this experience, you will have made progress in your desired outcomes. What led you to pick up this book? What do you want to learn from this experience? And most importantly, what actions are you willing to take to make your dreams a reality?

As you proceed to the next page, it's important to have an open mind. You will be introduced to information in unfamiliar ways. Our minds are constantly judging and labeling, which can take away from how we experience the world around us. I ask that you stay present and allow the new information to enter your awareness without trying to decide whether it is right or wrong, good or bad; it just is. Allow the information to seep in and flow through the channels of your mind and be open to where it leads you.

Remember:

"Minds are like parachutes—they only function when they're open."

—THOMAS DEWAR

"Be curious, not judgmental."

—WALT WHITMAN

Be willing to look at the people and events that happen in your life differently as well. Recognize that all the people who cross your path are there to help you create your BUS story; whether they are there to support you or to challenge you, they will test you, your abilities, and your beliefs, which will inevitably help your story to evolve.

I want to encourage you to enter this experience with your defenses down and your arms wide open, ready to receive all that awaits you. Though there may be times when hurt feelings arise, allow the pain or discomfort to come in as a way to understand where it originated and what it is trying to tell you about yourself.

Remember to question yourself and ask: "How is this person or situation helping me grow?" or "What can I learn from this situation to support me further in creating my BUS story?" Whether you have positive encounters or negative ones, you will grow from all the people and events that enter your story.

If your past belief has been that the universe is designed to see you fail, evolving is going to be difficult for you. You will see that once you have decided on a vision for your life, the universe will align with your thoughts and send the right people and opportunities to move you toward your goals.

Remember, as the writer of your story, you are the one holding the pencil; you are the one who writes your story. You say what happens, you pick the featuring characters, you say what the story teaches or does not teach, and your attitude and response to events and people in your life will determine how your story unfolds.

And finally...

Nothing happens by just reading about it. Think about this. If you read about how to boil an egg, does the egg boil? No, it does not. You must pick up the egg, place it in the water, and take steps to take the egg from its raw form to a cooked form. It is the same for life. Too often, we pick up great books that move us and make us think about growth and change, only to return to our old, unhelpful habits—our raw form.

It is important that as you read, you also make moves. There will be reflections and exercises that will guide your steps as you write your BUS story. This is because growth should happen in synergy with learning. As a former teacher, I learned the effect of combining lessons with immediate practice. Just like students, when we learn something new, it is best to try it out right away so the new learning can shape new habits and form new beliefs.

To add to what you will learn from your own and through your experiences, I am excited to share the lessons I've learned as well as what I've learned from others. My hope is that our stories will inspire you to write your story in your own words. Remember, no two stories are alike, but having the courage to share your story will give others the courage to share theirs.

I hope this book will serve as your personal guide to help you actually *do* something about the parts of your story you don't like or to examine past blockages in a new way that will help you to write your best BUS story!

Are you ready to get started? Grab your pencil, and let's go!

My Commitment:

My signature below confirms that I will enter this experience with an open mind. I will not only review and reflect on the content and lessons presented but also complete the exercises in the workbook located in the back of this book (or I will download a separate workbook at www.niki-spears.com). I am dedicated and committed to writing my best BUS story.

Signature: _____ Date: _____

1

BE Responsible 100%

"Strength and growth come only through continuous effort and struggle."
—Napoleon Hill

In August 2019, I was asked to be the keynote speaker for a convocation of a school district with approximately four thousand employees. The district was going through a lot of change as it was in the process of hiring a new superintendent and filling several other leadership positions. Since many of my presentations are centered around positivity, the planning committee, consisting of district leaders, thought it would be great to have me speak to the district employees about the power of positivity.

The planning committee and I scheduled several video conferences to talk about the theme for the event, goals, and other details. As with any event, I like to ensure my message is aligned with the district's overall strategy, and I want to make sure I weave in district goals and expectations into my presentation.

After listening to the planning committee talk about the uncertainty of having so many new leaders and how the changes were negatively impacting the district, I suggested I talk about creating a BUS story. Now, unlike you, they had not yet learned that this was an acronym, and they probably thought that I was talking about a physical bus. Nevertheless, they were intrigued by the theme of a BUS story, and of course, they wanted to know more.

I explained that a BUS story is when we discover the *beauty underneath the struggle*. It's when we lean into change and uncertainties to discover who we are and gain the courage to grow into who we are meant to be. Once I explained what a BUS story was, the committee became completely silent for several seconds. Finally, one of the members spoke up and said, "Niki, I don't think it's a good idea for you to mention the word 'struggle.' Our team is already going through a lot right now with all the changes, and I'm afraid that if you talk about struggles, it will be a reminder of all the negative things going on in the district, and we definitely don't need more negativity. We need you to talk about positivity."

The Beauty Underneath the Struggle

This got me to thinking—why do we associate conflict, challenges, or struggles with negativity? I proceeded with our discussion and asked the team to Google the definition of the word *struggle*. Several of the team members immediately took out their phones and recited the definition that was now staring them in the face.

"To make forceful or violent efforts to get free of restraint or constriction," one member read.

"To engage in conflict," another member added.

"To strive to achieve or attain something in the face of difficulty or resistance," the final member added.

"So who says a struggle is negative?" I asked. "Struggle is a part of the human experience; it is an action word that shows movement in the face of adversity. Until we change the way we see and experience our perceived struggles, we'll never have the ability to grow into the person, school, or district we were meant to be. Helping your team members learn to see the opportunities presented in the changes taking place in the district will help them focus their energy on what they *can do* rather than what they can't," I added.

After breaking down the meaning of struggle, not only did the team members invite me to talk about creating a BUS story during my keynote address, but they also invited me to participate in a breakout session that would allow me to dive deeper into the topic and to respond to employee questions about creating their BUS story.

I was so proud when several district leaders, teachers, and staff walked up to me after my presentation and asked if I had a book that would help them to write their own BUS stories. So here it is!

This book you're now holding is my gift to you. The energy to write the words you're reading has been in the waiting room of my mind, patiently delaying any action until just the right moment to unveil the secrets of how our daily challenges can hold amazing opportunities. This is because I despised and rejected my struggles for so long that I allowed them to have power over my happiness. I would first have to understand how these struggles could propel me to move into the life I intended to live. I know that this book wouldn't have come to life before this moment because I needed to grow and develop the courage to embrace all of my experiences, good and those I perceived as bad, to share this journey with you. It has taken me several years to look at things through a different set of lenses, to see how amazing opportunities are often disguised as struggles or challenges that lead us to our true purpose.

Any good book we've read or any great movie we've seen has an element of struggle: that conflict that keeps us reading or glued to the screen. So why would our own stories be any different? Our struggles define us and lead us to a higher purpose. For years, I felt absent of purpose because I shied away from my perceived struggles. When I experienced a struggle, I would slide into victim mode and throw a big pity party for myself. If I didn't get the job I wanted, if a relationship suddenly ended, or if other unfortunate things happened that didn't go as I intended, I would immediately feel sorry for myself.

One of the reasons I would take these mishaps so hard is because I associated them with my life purpose. I looked for purpose in what I was doing—a job, my position at home, or even the way others perceived me. It wasn't until I learned that purpose is less about *what* we do and more about *how* we do it that I was able to move beyond victimhood and have the courage to embrace losing a job or a relationship as a new opportunity.

I understand that my passion enables me to do what I've been called to do and not to question so much why something has happened but instead to look for what new experiences await. I believe that we are all inspired teachers of some subject. We were all created for a unique purpose. We all have a unique gift that is meant to be shared with others: that is the true purpose of our existence. No matter what chapter you're on in your story, I hope you are prepared to learn a little more about yourself as you create your BUS story.

Imagine you are holding a pencil. Not just any pencil, but one with strong lead and a durable eraser. As you study this pencil, think about its power and the possibilities it can bring. With this simple but remarkable instrument, you can draw, mark, color, or outline anything that has happened or will happen in your life. You can write something new, allowing more rewarding experiences to decorate the remaining pages of your story. You can write practically anything your heart desires: peaceful relationships with yourself and others, successful ventures and what you learned as a result, and even your legacy—what others will remember about you when you are no longer here.

Now, allow your attention to travel to the opposite end of the pencil to the eraser. With this resilient, rubbery tool, you can rub away marks you've made or even perceptions written in previous chapters such as negative stories, dysfunctional relationships, or interpretations. That's right, you can reinvent the experiences you've had over the years by telling yourself a different story. In other words, with one end of the pencil, you can write anything you want, and with the opposite end (the eraser), you can clean up anything you've written that doesn't align with where you want to be.

When you think about the capabilities of this pencil, you realize it's pretty awesome! The only thing that prevents you from connecting the pencil to a sheet of paper is your lack of courage to write something new.

This pencil you are holding is *you*.

"Start writing, no matter what. The water does not flow until the faucet is turned on."

—LOUIS L'AMOUR

As a motivational speaker, I often integrate the BUS story into my message because struggle is something we all have in common. If you are living on this planet, struggle is inevitable. Take the COVID-19 pandemic, for instance. It has forced the closure of our schools for the remainder of the year, restaurants and other small businesses have shut their doors, and many of us will be confined to our homes for several weeks, maybe even months. This is a struggle that any person in any part of the world can relate to; however, it's also an opportunity to create a BUS story as we challenge ourselves to find purpose in this moment. As I sit here confined to my home, unable to travel, I am now writing this book. Without this time, I'm not sure I would be writing at all. This is yet another of my BUS stories! Finding the beauty underneath the struggle.

I've witnessed some amazing BUS stories over the past several weeks. Teachers and principals are coming together, driving through their students' neighborhoods with signs and posters reminding them of how much they're missed and loved; restaurant owners transforming their businesses into food kitchens; and common people starting their own businesses to support those in need; and the list goes on. With every challenge comes great opportunity, and when we can look at struggles in this way, it can impact the outcome and provide our lives with greater meaning.

Our thoughts, our beliefs, and the stories we tell ourselves help shape who we are and our perceptions of self, people, and the world around us. Every detail of our being was created for a distinct purpose. Just like the pencil, every physical feature we have and all of our natural talents were designed for a specific purpose. When you are walking in purpose and you feel passionate about life, the pages of your story will naturally evolve.

A BUS Story

Early one weekday morning in March 2016, my husband and I headed to the gym for a quick workout before starting our day. We both worked in the same school district; I worked as an elementary school principal and Kermit as a chief human resources officer.

As I prepared to start my usual twenty-minute walk on the treadmill, I plugged my headphones into my cell phone and cranked up an inspirational message by Deepak Chopra, one of my favorite authors and a prominent figure in the New Age movement. Chopra talked about being intentional about the things we want out of life. He said that whatever you desire, you need to create a picture in your mind of yourself doing it.

I was at a point in my life where my heart and spirit yearned to do more. I had become a school principal because I wanted to impact lives in a much greater way outside the classroom. But after two years of being a principal, my school was beginning to feel like a small classroom; the walls seemed to be closing in, and I aspired to turn the page and start a new chapter.

Here was my struggle.

At the same time, two other things were going on. I had applied for a principal position at a high-needs campus in my district, and in my current school, I was dealing with a company that was threatening to sue us if my students and staff continued to use concepts from its book, which I had introduced two years earlier. Neither situation had anything to do with the other; however, I believe that without both struggles happening at once, one of my best BUS stories would never have evolved.

So since I refer to these events as my struggle, you can probably guess that I wasn't selected for the principal position on the high-needs campus, and in addition, I was told by our district attorney that we would need to stop using the concepts from the book that I had introduced. The latter was not going to be easy, as these principles had become a big part of our school culture. Students had embraced and were using the language, teachers had adopted the concepts and taught them in their classrooms, and we had just purchased banners and hallway signs that displayed all the principles from the book. Let's just say these concepts practically clothed the walls of our school building.

Now, back to the morning workout.

As Chopra shared his knowledge about being intentional about the things we desire, I allowed myself to think about what I really wanted for my life. I envisioned myself traveling to different schools and legally teaching the principles from the book I was told not to use. These concepts had been a game changer in both our school and my personal life, and I wanted to share them with the world. On the treadmill that morning, I took Chopra's advice and mentally created a picture of me standing in front of educators, sharing the message of these success principles and how they could transform each person within the school. That morning, I became intentional about what I wanted for my life.

Now here is the beauty of this struggle.

The Beauty Underneath the Struggle

After I did not get the job in my district, I decided to put my energy into keeping our school culture intact. We put together a committee consisting of teachers, staff, and students who would help devise an action plan of next steps we could take to save the culture we had created.

On Sunday, April 22, 2016, after returning home from dinner with Kermit, I remember staying behind in the car and aimlessly looking at my LinkedIn page.

As I scrolled and scrolled on LinkedIn, my thumb stopped on Jon Gordon's profile. Jon Gordon is a best-selling author, motivational speaker, and leader in creating positive culture. As I stared at Mr. Gordon's profile page, I heard a voice as clear as day say to me, "I want you to continue to take risks." At that moment, I knew exactly what the voice was directing me to do.

With my heart racing, I typed a quick message to Mr. Gordon:

Hi, Mr. Gordon! I am an elementary school principal and would love to work with you on putting together a curriculum for students to learn these valuable skills early in life! Let me know your thoughts! Take care.

Suddenly, I realized it wasn't a specific set of principles that had transformed our school culture; this change had happened because we had alignment. We had embraced the same values, goals, and beliefs. The principles we had been using could be replaced with something else. I sent that message to Mr. Gordon that Sunday evening, and I didn't tell anyone what I had done, not even Kermit.

The next morning, I went back to my LinkedIn page and noticed that I had a message from Mr. Gordon:

Thank you. Let me know what you had in mind more specifically. You can email me—Just a one pager of your thoughts would be great. Then we can talk. My cell is ###. We receive these requests often. I've been waiting for the right fit. Thank you so much for caring. Jon

"I've been waiting for the right fit" spoke to me in a spiritual way.

Later that evening, I sent Mr. Gordon that one pager and a couple of weeks later flew out to meet him to share my vision for creating and sustaining positive culture in our schools. During our meeting, Mr. Gordon explained he would allow me to do this; however, he couldn't pay me. My heart sank. Here I was ready for the opportunity of a lifetime, and there was no pay attached.

After I talked to my sweet husband about this opportunity, he encouraged me to go for it.

I recall him saying, "You'll always be able to go back and be a teacher or a principal, but you may never get this opportunity again."

I left my job as a principal at the end of that school year to pursue the vision I had in the gym that magical morning back in March, and the rest, my friends, is one of the best BUS stories I've ever created. Talk about being intentional!

I love sharing this story as I encourage people to embrace their struggles as they may never know what amazing opportunities await.

Although I left my job with no promise of pay, I believed in it so much that I took the risk, leaving behind my salary and my retirement. Along with the author Jon Gordon, I cofounded The Energy Bus for Schools Leadership Journey, a program that provides schools with training and coaching to create and sustain a positive culture. In addition to this, I am now a motivational speaker, sharing with audiences the power to transform their stories by using valuable principles and encouraging them to take 100 percent responsibility for their lives. You see, our BUS stories begin with a challenge, but when we push forward through the adversity accompanying the challenge, we find *the beauty underneath the struggle*.

Over a lifetime, we will experience and create several BUS stories. The one I described above is one of my favorites. I love sharing how I went from being a principal of one small school in Texas to being a leader of many schools across the country. Our BUS stories are more than the outcomes of our struggle; they involve making the conscious decision to be present in the moment and loving the process as it unfolds.

I've said it before, and I'll say it again, every good book you've read and every great movie you've seen will always have an element of conflict. It is that part of the story that draws us closer to the main characters as we witness them become the heroes, or the villains, of their stories. That doesn't mean just loving the parts that feel good, the parts that work. You must love it *all*! Love the hardships and the struggles. Love it because they are not failures; they are lessons that give you more of what you need to continue writing your story. When you can find the beauty underneath the struggle, you're not only growing as a person in these moments but also opening a world of opportunities that will give you the ability to step into what you were created to do.

You're Invited!

What if you were invited to a book-writing party? The book is being written in celebration of your life. Several of your friends and family members, even your boss and coworkers, have gathered to be a part of this celebration. One of your

The Beauty Underneath the Struggle

close family members is leading the celebration, and you are sitting proudly, waiting to see what happens next. After all, this is about you, right?

The family member who is leading the celebration quickly hands out pencils and paper and assigns each person a chapter to write in your story. The only person who does not receive a pencil or paper for the assignment is you. You look on quietly as everyone is writing, discussing, and sharing ideas about your life and the way they think your story should go. You try to engage a few times, yet no one is listening. You even try to grab a pencil and a sheet of paper, but they have all been handed out. It looks like everyone is having a great time planning your story. You are beginning to hate this party and feel left out of your own life.

Do you ever feel like this? Like your life story is being written by others.

If you are feeling like other people or events in your life have more say-so about what happens in your story than you, then you are not the writer of your story. For you to live your best life and create brilliant BUS stories, you will have to tell your writing-party attendees to pack up and go home! You will have to take the pages of your life and write them yourself. You will have to take 100 percent responsibility for everything at this moment, even the parts of your story you have allowed others to write about you. You must realize you were the one who sat back and allowed this to happen.

Wake Up! Own 100 Percent of Your Story!

A couple of years ago, one of my friends sent me one of Will Smith's inspirational videos. You guys know Will, the actor, songwriter, and rapper, the "Fresh Prince of Bel-Air"! Yes, that Will! My friend sent me the video and suggested we use it for one of our trainings.

In the video, Will shares the difference between fault and responsibility. He says, "It don't matter whose fault it is that something is broken if it's your responsibility to fix it." He continues:

It's not somebody's fault if their father was an abusive alcoholic, but it's for damn sure their responsibility to figure out how they are going to deal with those traumas and make a life out of it. It's not your fault if your partner cheated and ruined your marriage, but it is for damn sure your responsibility to figure out how to take that pain and how to overcome that and build a happy life for yourself. Fault and responsibility do not go together; it sucks. When something is somebody's fault, we want them to suffer, we want them punished, we want them to pay, we want it to be their responsibility to fix it, but that's not how it works...As long as we are pointing the finger...we are jammed and trapped into victim mode. When you are in victim mode, you are stuck in suffering. [The] road to power is in taking responsibility. Your heart. Your life. Your happiness.

Will added one more thing at the end of the video: "Taking responsibility, accepting responsibility, is not an admission to guilt. You're not admitting you're at fault...it's a recognition of power that you seize when you stop blaming people."[1] Wow! Well said, Will! To write your BUS story, you must wake up and realize that your story is your responsibility. I don't know any great writers who can actually write while sleeping; writing requires action, and movement requires responsibility. If you're going to experience an awakening, you must first realize that right now you are asleep. That's right, even when you are walking around your home or your workplace, or you are out with family and friends, there are some parts of you that have not been awakened,

---

[1] Will Smith, "Fault vs Responsibility, YouTube video, WhateverIt TakesMotivation, posted on January 31, 2018, YouTube video, 2:29, https://www.youtube.com/watch?v=USsqkd-E9ag.

that reside in your unconscious mind, controlling many aspects of yourself that you may not be aware of and that could be holding you back from writing your story.

Uninvite Yourself from the Victim Party

For many years of my life, I was asleep. I did not understand how my unconscious mind was directing my beliefs. I was a blamer and a complainer, and I couldn't see how my behavior was impacting me as well as those around me. I never realized this behavior kept me at a level of victimhood, scribbling on a blank sheet of paper, and prevented me from turning to the next page or chapter of my life. You see, many of your beliefs about yourself and your life are hidden within your unconscious mind. I learned that if real change was going to happen, I had to shift my thinking. I would have to let go of blaming others and take responsibility for everything that had happened in my life. Let's face it, success has little to do with what happens externally; it's really what's happening on the inside, our mindset, which determines our destiny. Unless we are willing to release ourselves from placing fault or blame on others, we will continue to block the blessings that are meant to flow into our lives. Taking responsibility for where we are now can be challenging, especially when you've experienced trauma or other unfortunate situations.

I Woke Up!

My awakening happened in June 2010. I'll never forget it. I was in my home office, sitting in my comfy chair, drinking a cup of coffee, when Kermit entered the room, insisting that I read the first page of some book he was holding. Kermit is an avid reader, always discovering something new, and he is often excited to share his new learnings with me. In my story, he has been the helper, someone who possesses magical powers and helps the main characters to accomplish their goals.

As I glanced at the book he held, I thought to myself, there is no way in hell I'm reading all of that (the book had to have about a thousand pages)! Kermit, knowing the avid reader I had not become, followed up immediately in his most excited voice, "Just read the first page, that's it!" I looked at the book again and took it from his hands with the hope he would leave me alone to enjoy my morning cup of coffee.

The book, by Jack Canfield and Janet Switzer, was titled *The Success Principles. How to Get from Where You Are to Where You Want to Be.* The title of the first section is "Take 100% Responsibility for Your Life," and below is a summary of the first page.

One of the most pervasive myths in American culture today is that we are *entitled* to a great life—that somehow, somewhere, someone (certainly not us) is responsible for filling our lives with continual happiness, exciting career options, nurturing family time, and blissful personal relationships simply because we exist.

But the real truth—and the one lesson the whole book is based on—is that there is only one person responsible for the quality of the life you live.

That person is *you*.

If you want to be successful, you must take 100 percent responsibility for everything that you experience in your life. This includes the level of your achievements, the results you produce, the quality of your relationships, the state of your health and physical fitness, your income, your debts, your feelings—everything!

This is not easy.

In fact, most of us have been conditioned to blame something outside ourselves for the parts of our life we don't like. We blame our parents, our bosses, our friends, the media, our coworkers, our clients, our spouse, the weather, the economy, our astrological chart, our lack of money— anyone or anything we can pin the blame on. We never want to look at where the real problem is—ourselves.[2]

---

[2] Jack Canfield and Janet Switzer, *The Success Principles: How to Get from Where You Are to Where You Want to Be* (New York: HarperCollins Publishers, 2005), 3.

The Beauty Underneath the Struggle

On this day, sitting in my comfy chair, with my coffee in hand, I woke up. All this time, I had never realized I was a blamer. I didn't even realize I was giving others power over my story as I blamed external forces and people for the things in my life I didn't like. I didn't realize that taking responsibility would become my greatest superpower, the one thing that would tremendously change the direction of my life, my story. On this day, I took the pencil from my parents, my siblings, my friends, my bosses, and all those unfortunate events I'd experienced. For the first time, I was ready to write my own story.

Now when I speak to audiences of educators, leaders, and even students, I always share my awakening and read the first page from *The Success Principles*. As I am reading and I observe the faces in the audience, I can literally feel people waking up, just as I did over ten years ago. After each presentation, there is always one person (sometimes more) who will approach me and ask if he or she can snap a cell phone picture of the first page of the book or who simply wants me to remind them of the title and the author.

A feeling of empowerment comes along with taking 100 percent responsibility for your story. If you haven't tried it yet, I invite you to do so now. It's accompanied by this feeling of being in control, not necessarily of everything that takes place in your life, but it definitely lends you the power to *choose* how you will respond to your perceived struggles. When you reach this level of consciousness, you are no longer controlled by external circumstances. You are at the beginning stages of seeing the beauty underneath any struggle.

Commit to change now!

Your turn! Ready to take 100 percent responsibility?

Go to the workbook and complete the exercise for Chapter 1: **BE** Responsible -100%

2

BE Aware

"Decide what your truth is. Then live it."
—KAMAL RAVIKANT

Whose truth are you living right now? If you're going to create a good BUS story, you will need to find the courage to live your truth. This can be challenging. When we are young, we attend what I like to call "family belief camp." It happens the moment we are born: we enter a training camp in which we are taught our families' beliefs and values—how to label and respond to people, things, and situations in our lives. This training goes on for several years, and some of us are still enrolled today and have never graduated.

In this belief camp, we watch the adults and the way they manage themselves, and we model our behaviors after theirs. Because many of us want to please our caregivers, we suspend our own choices in exchange for a stronger sense of connection with them. We usually feel good about ourselves when we are doing something that pleases them, and we feel bad when our behaviors are not acceptable. During our time in family belief camp, we learn how to reject our truth for *their truth*. So how do we drill down to determine our truth? And what can we do about negative beliefs that are impacting our emotional well-being? I'll answer both!

Scroll all the way down!

To reconnect with your truth, you will need to tap into your core beliefs, those views and opinions you learned and accepted during your time in family belief camp. The home you live in right now has a certain shape and height because of its foundation; you have certain views and opinions because of your background, your foundation.

Let's look at our life like a social media page with endless scrolling. When you scroll downward, you can view the events of the past, and if you scroll back up and refresh the page, you are back on the current page, where you can post current thoughts or events. So how do you identify your core values? Pick one of your actions or monumental decisions, or even just one aspect of your character. Open it like a tab in your browser and scroll all the way down through the years until you find its foundation. You are the way you are, not because of something that just happened, but because of different influences over the years.

Follow the Why!

Our core beliefs about ourselves, others, and the world can restrict us from believing or becoming the people we were meant to be. We may have never considered where or how they drive us, but they do. When we adopt a belief, we will go through life gathering evidence to support the belief as our truth. This can be damaging to our growth, especially when the belief is negative. Some of the common beliefs I had growing up were that people can't be trusted, the world is a dangerous place, and most people don't like you because they are jealous. Because I accepted these beliefs as my truth, all these things tended to show up in my relationships, my jobs, and even my home.

Whether I realized it or not, many of my behaviors centered around my core beliefs. For example, because I chose to believe that the world was a dangerous place, I was reluctant to take risks and worried a lot about something happening to me or my family.

There is a core belief in the background of every decision we make, every action we take, and every path we follow. We have beliefs about what we can or cannot accomplish based on our beliefs about ourselves, and our actions are an indication of what we have accepted as our truth. It's important to take some time to consider some of our core beliefs so we can create new stories to replace those that bring us fear, worry or grief and reinforce the stories that have served us well.

Now, pick one of the core beliefs you have identified, and let's scroll down to the source. I will share one of my beliefs as an example for you as you determine the source of your own. Please note, beliefs are not always negative; it's also important to understand where your positive beliefs originated so that you can begin inviting more positive experiences into your life.

Start by picking a thought that is constant or reoccurring in your mind. A thought that has constantly haunted me is, "If I don't work hard, I will fail and be unable to support myself and my family financially."

So let's uncover where this thought originated. Follow the thread of that thought, all the way down until you find the time when it was first posted on your time line. Ask yourself, "Why do I feel this way?" You will find an answer like, "You must work hard to succeed." Ask another "why" question. Like a detective, continue to ask yourself *why* until you get closer to the root of the belief, for instance,

"I fear having to rely on others for support." Once you've uncovered the emotion related to the belief, ask another why question—Why do you fear relying on others' support? You will find, like I did, that there is a reason behind every response. Follow it all the way back until you understand your beliefs enough to navigate them. This process helped me to identify an underlying belief about myself of which I was unaware.

When I was a kid, and my parents had disagreements, I would overhear my father tell my mother that everything belonged to him—the money, the cars, even the house we were living in. And I would watch my mom shrink as if this were true. Although I'm sure this was said out of anger, as a young girl, I felt helpless and insecure.

After applying the "Follow the Why" process, I have a better understanding of why I fear losing a job or not being able to support myself financially. This belief was a result of how I perceived the relationship between a man and a woman growing up: if you didn't want to depend on others to support you financially, you would have to work hard. My internal receptors connected these moments to feelings of unworthiness and not measuring up.

As I got older, I learned that each of us has our own internal reader that provides us with feedback about the things that are taking place around us. And just like beliefs, perceptions are not real and should always be questioned. I would never have come to this conclusion about this belief if I had not had the courage to be vulnerable and revisit those feelings I had as a child. So it's important to identify the belief, but it's just as important to have the courage to follow the thread and venture back to wherever it may lead.

Now it's your turn! Go to the workbook and complete the first exercise for Chapter 2: **BE** Aware.

Your Beliefs, Your Story

Your larger story has been shaped by several smaller stories, and sometimes, you need to transform a few of these smaller stories before you create new ones. You cannot control what others have said about you, but you can control the views you choose to become part of your belief system, your truth. The best way to discover negative beliefs about yourself or others is to pay close attention to themes in your thinking. If, in various situations, you tend to focus on negative things about work or home or even on a trip to the grocery store, then a negative core belief about yourself is probably at work.

Start today using the eraser on your pencil to erase the negative stories you've accepted and tell yourself different stories. Instead of telling yourself, "I am not worthy," simply say, "I am worthy!" But saying it is only the first step; you must believe it! Think of all the great qualities you possess and tell yourself positive stories to reinforce your truth.

Our core beliefs are not only presented through our family belief camp but also influenced by our culture, society, environment, region, and even biology. These patterns of thinking influence our perceptions and our attitudes toward the people and things around us. When we believe something, we accept it as our truth. We come to believe since the things and people around us are this way, we have no choice but to be that way as well. But this is not true. When we question our beliefs, then and only then can we step outside these opinions and ask ourselves if these beliefs are serving us in a positive way.

When my girls were younger, I took them to see a movie called *The Jungle Book*. Mowgli, the main character in the story, is raised by a pack of wolves, and so he believes that he is also a wolf, just a less hairy version. This is because Mowgli attended the wolves' family belief camp for several years of his life. Just like Mowgli's, our experiences form our personality, which then becomes an important part of our story. Piece by piece, one word after another, the things we hear (and observe) form our belief system.

Expanding Our Beliefs

Beliefs and perceptions should not be static; just as our bodies expand and grow, our beliefs should expand as well. If new principles are going to enter our belief system, we must first be willing to tell ourselves new stories about the things happening in our lives. We may have a difficult time transforming these stories because this means we must also take responsibility for our current beliefs and the consequences of embracing these beliefs. As you create your BUS story, let go and reframe beliefs that do not serve you well so that new understandings can enter your writing process.

So can we choose our beliefs?

The answer is yes. We may not be able to choose the events that take place in our lives, but our stories take shape based on how we respond to these situations, which can directly impact our larger story.

To expand your beliefs, do the following:

1. First, repeat the "Follow the Why" exercise often and identify your belief and how it makes you feel.
2. If it is a belief that is not serving you well, tell yourself a different story. For example, instead of saying, "I am not worthy," simply say, "I am worthy!"
3. Provide evidence of what makes you worthy, your awesomeness.

4. Accept your belief and repeat it daily.
5. Take action to support your new beliefs. Changing your behavior will reinforce your new belief. Give yourself permission to do things you love doing, accept compliments from others, have fun, and stop taking yourself so seriously.

Remember, you do not have to be who your environment says you are. You do not have to be who your teacher said you are. You don't even have to be who your mother tells you that you are. *We all get to choose.*

*Go to Chapter 2 of the workbook titled ~**BE** Aware and review the Positive Thinking Model and how beliefs are adopted.*

Every Experience, Every Thought Matters

I had the opportunity to talk to Julie Ward Nee, my friend and the head of training for Jon Gordon Companies. From the moment I first spoke with Julie on the phone, I knew that she had amazing energy and a beautiful spirit. Just the sound of her voice radiates a sense of peace that all is right with the world.

I interviewed Julie for this book because a couple of years ago, her struggle was shared with the rest of our team when we learned of her cancer diagnosis. I admired Julie's vulnerability with what was happening to her as she lost her hair and, eventually, her eyelashes and eyebrows. I was drawn to her courage as I watched her continue to travel and conduct training, still giving her participants her best. But what I really wanted her to share with us is how she found beauty during those tough times. What was it about her belief system that helped her create this amazing BUS story?

Julie's parents divorced when she was seven years old, and this impelled her to become more independent. At an early age, she helped with chores, cleaned the house, and even mowed the lawn to help her single mom. By the age of thirteen, she had her own paper route, and as she got older, she worked in retail. I think it's safe to say that Julie was a very responsible child, which she attributes to her self-reliance and self-confidence. Her mother nurtured these qualities in her, and she describes her mom as being super open, loving, and supportive. In Julie's words, "She thought I hung the moon." Her mother was a positive person who taught Julie to believe in herself. Julie's core values and belief system have helped her throughout her life. She says that because she had a mom who always told her "If you can see it, you can create it," she adopted that as part of her belief system. So it's no surprise that this belief helped Julie during her fight with cancer. Instead of focusing on what she couldn't do, she turned her focus on the things that were going well. She would often remind herself, "One glass of water at a time."

The stories you are told, the sights you see, and the things you read make up different ideas and beliefs in your mind, and each of these beliefs is like a building block. One is placed over the other, and another over that one, to form who we are. Julie's story is a beautiful example of how these beliefs can help you in moments of struggle. Julie learned early that with a positive attitude as a weapon, you can defeat anything—even cancer!

Julie (right) and her mother, Beverly

Your Beliefs Will Guide Your Why

"The two most important days in life are the day you are born, and the day you discover the reason why."
—MARK TWAIN

A man and his young family traveled down a highway on a summer road trip. Three miles outside the nearest small town, traffic slowed to a crawl, then completely stopped. Frustrated, the man searched his phone for the cause of the traffic. Was it an accident or some other catastrophic event that was causing bumper-to-bumper traffic in a rural area so early in the afternoon? Finding no reason for the pileup, he flagged down an officer who was busy directing traffic and asked. "Funeral," the officer said. Well, that didn't make any sense to the man. There had to be hundreds of cars in line, and he couldn't imagine a person, important enough to command this type of procession, could be from this small rural American town.

"Who died, a billionaire?"

The officer turned to him again, misty-eyed. "No, the custodian from the middle school. For thirty years, she loved on our kids."

Believe it or not, some people believe that a school custodian leads a less-than-impactful existence. Oftentimes, we are judged based on our financial achievements in life, and those who fare better financially are perceived to live a better life. This is simply not true. The secret to leading a fulfilling life is not about what you make in life but about what you make out of life.

What would you like to be remembered for?

"Everyone has been made for some particular work, and the desire for that work has been put in every heart."

—Jalaluddin Rumi

When I was a little girl, I often envisioned myself being on stage, singing. I can still see the stage in my childhood dreams and all the people who came out to see me perform. It wasn't necessarily the fame that interested me in becoming an entertainer, but the opportunity to bring joy and happiness to others. When people like Michael Jackson, Whitney Houston, or other talented singers lit up my television screen, I felt an abundance of joy, excitement, and jubilation. I wanted to be a part of the magic that was happening. I would often look into the faces of the audiences on the television and notice how happy they were; there was no grief or sadness, only smiles. I begin to see entertaining others as a way of getting rid of sadness and making people happy, and this came naturally for me.

When my relatives came to our house for a visit, I wanted to provide them with that magical feeling I had when I watched my favorite singers perform. Even though I lacked the bright lights and stage, I sang, told stories and jokes, and did other crazy shenanigans that brought laughter and joy to their faces—my relatives became my audience. That same entertainer mindset followed me as an adult into my career. As a teacher, my students became my audience, and as a principal, my entire school became my audience. To me, creating a dynamic culture means bringing joy, excitement, and jubilation to every person within my reach so that he or she feels valued and appreciated.

Today I travel all over the country, speaking to educators, principals, parents, students, and superintendents about the importance of creating and sustaining positive cultures in our schools. Even though I'm not literally singing, as I envisioned as a child, I do something even better: I use my voice to inspire people to create the lives of their dreams by taking ownership of their stories.

My purpose statement: I exist to inspire and challenge others to find their purpose so that they will share more happiness, joy, and peace with others.

The Beauty Underneath the Struggle

What is your purpose?

If we want to know our purpose, we will need to look beyond our ego and self to discover why we exist. We can become detached from our purpose because the world tells us that a great life has to do with what we have accomplished or how we are perceived by others. If we're not popular, famous, or rich, we may feel that we're not fulfilling our purpose.

We start our day by looking in the mirror. We check our reflection throughout the day to make sure every hair is in place and that our appearance is perfect. We flip through dozens of group pictures of ourselves or selfies, searching for the one that paints us in the best light physically. What we're not so eager to do is open our hearts to those natural gifts that make us feel fulfilled and happy. Your purpose can be as simple as bringing joy to others or having a sense of humor; whatever it is, allow that gift to flow from your heart and not from your head.

If you're unsure why you exist, you may need to spend time alone to uncover what has been buried in your heart. It will take courage to go into the deepest parts of yourself and discover your light, your true purpose.

Let's start now.

In my trainings and workshops, I will often ask participants to reflect on their *why*—their purpose for being.

I remind them that one of the reasons we become frustrated with work and life, in general, is because we lose sight of our purpose. Our purpose is what drives us when we're feeling down, as it lifts us to a higher level. We leave behind the ego and self to connect with our inner spirit.

I've always felt that there was something more I should be doing, and I often related this yearning to getting a high-level position in an organization; I used to associate my purpose with a job or a career. I always thought that the more I achieved in an organization, the more purposeful I would feel; this was not true. I found that the achievements I made in my career were short-lived. I would be happy when I got a new job or a promotion, but that happiness would soon fade, and I would start looking for the next job or promotion.

I've since discovered that when you have purpose, you feel alive, passionate, and clear. You're not concerned about the time, because you are totally absorbed in what you are doing. My first role in education was as a preschool teacher for Head Start. Before accepting this position, I had never imagined becoming a teacher. I had always thought I would be this glamorous businesswoman who traveled the world.

I remember being in my preschool classroom and being so engaged that I wouldn't even recognize it was time for my students to pack up and go home. I felt so passionate about what I was doing, I never even noticed the time. This was the first sign that education was my true calling.

Think about people who are in jobs or careers that may not provide good pay or benefits, yet they are passionate about their roles and the difference they make in the lives of others. Think about the school custodian example provided earlier in this chapter: for thirty years, she made children feel valued. She didn't see her work as just a job; it was her calling. When you look at what you're doing (work, family, relationships) as your calling, this is when you know you're living your *why*.

What are you naturally good at? What brings a smile to your face? What would you be doing if there was no concern about pay? If these questions are difficult for you to answer, think back to when you were a child. Consider things you took pleasure in that you still enjoy doing today. Take some time to reflect on these questions now in your workbook, and we'll see you back here as we prepare to discuss your vision.

Your turn! Go to Chapter 2: **BE** Aware of your workbook titled ~*Discovering Your Gifts* and complete the exercise.

Your Why

Now that you have a purpose statement, write it down and put it in a place where you can see it every day. Once you identify why you were created, you must then decide how you will use your gifts to serve others. Whether your purpose is to make positive connections with others, fight for a particular cause, or inspire a love for something in others, it will take courage to create a vision for the journey ahead. Robin Sharma, a Canadian writer best known for his book *The Monk Who Sold His Ferrari*, said, "Everything is created twice—first in the mind and then in reality." The house you live in, the building you work in, the bridge you drive across every day—all existed first in someone's mind. My dad will often tell us about his life as a young child and how he would go out to a pond and sit for hours and envision the life that he wanted to have. He said that when he looks at his life today, it is exactly what he dreamed about sitting at that pond over sixty years ago.

To put your purpose into action, you will first need to know what you want to accomplish. In our day-to-day routines, we can become so distracted by all the things that must be done that we forget about our own plans for our life. Having a set of goals will keep you focused and give you direction as you find ways to use your gift to serve others. In 2011, after I read *The Success Principles* by Jack Canfield (yes, I ended up reading the entire book), Kermit and I decided to create a goal book. In his book, Canfield suggests taking a binder or scrapbook and creating a separate goal on

The Beauty Underneath the Struggle

each page. He recommends that as new goals and desires emerge, you should add them to your goal book. Kermit and I took a composition book and did exactly that! On a separate page in the goal book, we wrote down our deepest desires. I decided to take it a step further and promised myself that every time a goal was achieved, I would write the date and how it felt to accomplish that goal. One of the goals that I wrote at that time was written on July 26, 2011. I had recently earned my principalship certification from the University of Texas at Austin and was serving as an intervention teacher in the Pflugerville Independent School District (PISD). My passion was to get more experience in school leadership, so the goal I wrote in my goal book was: *To be in a leadership role by August 2011 in Pflugerville ISD.*

I completed the district application to be considered for leadership positions, and on July 6, 2011, I received a call from the principal of an elementary school in Pflugerville, extending me an opportunity to interview with his team! I couldn't contain my excitement. I believe the principal knew and everyone around me knew I was excited because I literally screamed into the phone. At the time I was visiting my parents in Karnack, Texas, so I couldn't wait to return home and prepare for the interview.

I studied the school report cards, put together a presentation, and made interview packets for each member of the interview committee. I also drove by the school and just imagined myself being part of the school family. Finally, I snapped a picture with my cell phone and said to myself: "You will be the new assistant principal at this school!"

On July 11, the day of the interview, I killed it! I was so on point in the interview and was so impressed by the way I responded to every single question. I could tell the interview committee loved me, too; they seemed to laugh, nod in agreement, and smile at my responses. At the end, they asked me if I had questions for them. I asked each one of them to share one thing that they had learned about me that they believed would be a great asset to their school (this is a great question to see if the committee thinks your skills are a good fit and an awesome way to end the interview)! At the conclusion of the interview, the principal practically walked me out of the building and to my car. I knew I had this! I went home and waited for the phone call.

Well there was no phone call. The next day, I received an email from the principal stating that the committee had decided to move forward with another candidate and thanking me for my time. I was shocked. I stared at the message for several seconds; there had to be some mistake. I deleted the email. I don't know why; I just did. For some reason I had convinced myself that the job was mine and I wasn't going to allow this message to change what was in my heart.

The Beauty Underneath the Struggle

A few days later, on July 20, I received a call from a strange number: 400-10. It was the superintendent's office, and the lady on the other end of the phone wanted to schedule a meeting with me and the superintendent regarding my interview at the school. What could this possibly be about? I guess I would have to wait and find out.

With great anticipation I attended that meeting with the superintendent of schools, Charles Dupre, on July 26. When I walked into Mr. Dupre's office, I was met with great intimidation. Not only was I about to talk to the person that led the entire district but his office was humongous!

He invited me to have a seat and started with a little small talk. I don't recall anything that was said until he changed the course of the conversation and asked: "So are you ready to be an assistant principal?" I couldn't believe what I was hearing. Had they made a mistake? What was happening?

Mr. Dupre went on to explain that the number of students on the campus had increased for this year. He informed me that I was number two on the candidate list of five, and due to the numbers, they would need to hire not one assistant principal but two! And since I was number two, he wanted to offer me the job! He also told me that he doesn't hire assistant principals and he would expect that if I accepted the role, I would become a principal.

On July 26, 2011, just a few weeks after writing this goal, my dream became a reality.

Since that time, Mr. Dupre and I have worked in various capacities together including Fort Bend Independent School District, where I kept my promise and served as principal. I appreciate his leadership and am grateful that God brought us together.

While flipping through my old goal book the other day, I noticed several other accomplishments have come to pass that I will need to go back and update. I encourage you to take a notebook and title it *My Purpose Plan*, *My Goal Book*, or some other creative title of your choice. Do just as we did, and at the top of each page, write a goal you want to accomplish. Include as much information about the goal as possible. I would also recommend adding a date that you set the goal as it's great to see how long it will take to come to pass. Make sure your goals are related to things you want to happen in your life. Remember to write down as many goals as you can think of and check in with yourself each week to see how you are progressing. If you have a trusted friend or relative who will support you in accomplishing your goals, make him or her your accountability partner. Dr. Gail Matthews, a professor in the Department of Psychology at Dominican University, recruited 267 people from various businesses and organizations to participate in a study on goal achievement in the workplace. The study looked at how goal achievement is influenced by writing goals, committing to goal-directed actions, and accountability for those actions. Participants ranged in ages from twenty-three to seventy-two and represented different backgrounds. Matthews found that more than 70 percent of participants in her study reached their goals when they wrote them down and shared weekly progress with a friend.[3]

If your goal is to become a best-selling author, it will be helpful to create measurable goals that will help you to achieve this outcome. For example, you may create a goal of getting up at five o'clock in the morning to write for two hours each day. You could extend this goal to writing a specific number of words or pages during that two-hour period. This is a measurable goal because it is easy for you (and your accountability partner) to determine if your goals were accomplished based on the specifications you outlined for yourself. I always look at goals as actions, and if you can't actually see yourself doing it, then it's not a goal; it's just an idea!

Your turn! What goals would you like to achieve? Turn to your workbook and complete the exercise for Chapter 2: **BE** Aware~ *"Discovering Your Gifts.""*

---

[3] John Traugott, "Achieving Your goals: An Evidence-Based Approach," Michigan State University, August 26, 2014, https://www.canr.msu.edu/news/achieving_your_goals_an_evidence_based_approach.

Identifying Your Writing Style
Beliefs + Your Why = *You*

Writing your BUS story can be challenging if you haven't yet determined what kind of writer you are. Now that you are familiar with your core beliefs and you understand why you're here, let's take a look at your current writing style so that you can determine where you would like to be.

I came across the work of Dr. David R. Hawkins, a well-known psychiatrist, physician, and researcher and the author of *Power vs. Force* about a year ago. Since then, I've been sharing Hawkins's Map of Consciousness during my keynotes and workshops as a way to help people become more self-aware.

Hawkins's research reveals, "In this interconnected universe, every improvement we make in our private world improves the world at large for everyone. We all float on the collective level of consciousness of mankind so that any increment we add comes back to us. We all add to our common buoyancy by our efforts to benefit life. It is a scientific fact that what is good for you is good for me."[4] This means that each one of us can be acclimated to an energy level.

---

[4] David R. Hawkins, *Power vs. Force: The Hidden Determinants of Human Behavior* (Carlsbad: Hay House, 2012), 150.

The Beauty Underneath the Struggle

The map of consciousness is a hierarchical framework that illustrates the ladder of consciousness. From low to high, Hawkins describes the levels as shame, guilt, apathy, grief, fear, desire, anger, pride, courage, neutrality, willingness, acceptance, reason, love, joy, peace, and enlightenment.

Hawkins documented these consciousness levels on a scale from one to one thousand. On this scale, two hundred, the level of courage, is when we begin to add energy to everything around us. Below two hundred, we are net consumers of energy, meaning we are living in guilt, apathy, grief, fear, desire, anger, or pride.

One of the most fascinating parts of Hawkins's research is that approximately 85 percent of the people living today calibrate at low energy levels, below two hundred (courage) and that in a lifetime, many of us will never reach two critical points on the scale—level two hundred (courage) and level five hundred (love). He describes courage (level two hundred) as a positive state in which we feel empowered and capable and have a zest for life and love (level five hundred) as a state of being in service to others and having the ability to love self and others unconditionally. Another significant part of Hawkins's research is the power of one person's energy. He states that one person who is operating in the higher energy levels can have an enormous impact on many people who are in the low-level energy fields. For example, he notes:

One individual who lives and vibrates to the energy of optimism and willingness to be nonjudgmental of others will counterbalance the negativity of 90,000 individuals who calibrate at the lower weakening levels.[5]

Our energy is contagious, and it can impact others and greatly influence how our story unfolds. To help you develop your BUS story, I've developed a writer's style chart. Look at the descriptions below and determine what type of writer you are right now and where you aspire to be by the end of our journey together.

---

[5] Hawkins, *Power vs. Force*, 282.

The Beauty Underneath the Struggle

Writer's Style Chart
Where are you right now?

The chart below describes five types of writers. In a lifetime, you will move in and out of these levels. The goal is to notice where you reside most often as you choose where you want to be.

Love Story
This writer believes that love is unchanging. A love for self and others is unconditional. This person believes that we are better together. He knows that if one person wins, we all win. The sole purpose of his story is to inspire others to tell theirs.

Comedy
This writer sees life as enjoyable, unattached to outcomes. He doesn't take himself, people, or events that happen in his story personally. He sees life as a big opportunity to make a difference.

Rebirth/Awakening
This writer realizes that *he* is the author of his story. He is no longer blaming and complaining, but feeling empowered to take 100 percent responsibility for his story (his decisions, actions, behaviors, and results).

Drama/Action
This writer is driven by conflict and has a strong identification to the ego. This writer believes that the world should conform to him. His anger/frustration will often move him beyond the victim (no action) to being fueled to take action.

Horror
This writer is tied up into emotional energy of shame, guilt, fear, and despair, which ultimately makes him the victim of his story. This type of writer is not the writer at all as he allows others (and events) to dictate how his story should go.

© Niki Spears 2020

As you read through the descriptions, it will be clear that some or all these styles have applied to you at some point in time. Keep in mind that these stages are fluid; you will move in and out of these styles as you experience life. The goal here is to consider where your energy resides most of the time.

If you are constantly writing horror stories, then you may be residing at a level of victimhood, and when you're a victim, you have no authority over your story because you are allowing other people or circumstances to hold the pencil. When you can rise to a level of rebirth/awakening, you feel empowered and a renewed sense of freedom, as you begin to take ownership for your life and have the courage to move forward to write your masterpiece.

Their Story is not Your Story

"Be Yourself. Everyone else is already taken."
—OSCAR WILDE

Have you ever had to take a test or do an individual assignment in a class, and each time you look behind to see what your classmates are doing, you get stuck? You get stuck not because you lack the ideas and knowledge to continue the work, but because a glance at another person's work

The Beauty Underneath the Struggle

influences your thoughts and imagination, which can cause you to question yourself.

For so many people, this is the journey of their life; while they are sitting at their desks writing, they are stealing glances at another person's story, unable to focus on their own gifts and talents. Every story is unique. If your story was like everyone else's story, you wouldn't be the exceptional person you are. Your story is different from the stories of your siblings, friends, parents, and every other person living on earth. If you do not realize your story is meant to be different and specific to you alone, you may live your whole life according to someone else's script, and you will end up frustrated.

As the writer, you have the power to decide how your story will go. It does not matter the opinion of other characters in the story or even the reader; all that matters is the writer's opinion.

Commit to change now!

3

BE Open

"Struggles are doorways for miracles to enter.
—NIKI SPEARS *"*

Keshun Brown, my first cousin and one of my closest friends, has always been a model of positivity for me. I've watched her go through many struggles—a divorce, losing her job and her home, and most recently, losing her mom (my sweet aunt). Through all these struggles, the only thing that seems to stand out when I think of my cousin is her warm smile. So it's no surprise that Keshun is someone I wanted to interview for this book, as I was curious to learn what keeps her going when things around her seem to be falling apart.

Keshun attributes her high self-esteem and her positive attitude to both her parents. She said that although her dad was strict and a little traditional in his ways, he showered her with affection. Her mother was not as affectionate, but she knew that her mom loved her. She stated that the two balanced each other.

Her parents always made her feel like she was enough; this is why she is confident and happy in her skin. When I asked how she manages to stay positive when faced with so many obstacles, she attributes her resiliency to her faith in God. She says that she believes that God equipped her at a very young age for this life and prepared her for all the struggles she's faced.

I remember when her mom passed, and my daughter and I traveled down to visit my aunt prior to her funeral. I was in shock, and I had a difficult time seeing my aunt lying there, now absent of the life she had shared with me and so many. Instead of Keshun thinking of herself, she was comforting others and allowing grieving family members, like me, to cry on her shoulders. I finally had the opportunity to ask Keshun how she was able to do this. Her response, although simple in nature, was so insightful: she said it hurt her to see her people hurt. By putting others before herself, Keshun was able to find meaning in her mom's passing.

What if we all put others before ourselves? This is truly the secret to expanding your life and finding

The Beauty Underneath the Struggle

Keshun and her mom, Gloria

meaning. I often say that we were not placed on this earth to serve ourselves. When we are self-absorbed, we become stressed and frustrated, but when we understand that we were created to serve others, somehow our world opens and we feel awake and alive. Don't believe me? Try it. The next time you're feeling depressed or stressed, try doing something for someone else and watch how sharing your love and compassion becomes an invitation to welcome more of the same into your own life.

Like Keshun, I believe that we were equipped for a life of struggle. The key is to understand that our struggles are not meant to destroy us but to help us to grow and to prepare for a life of resiliency.

There will be struggles that stand in the way of you writing your story, and once you understand some of these blockages and how to move past them, you will be prepared to handle anything that comes your way. First, knowing that there is a higher power that is working in your favor, you suddenly realize that you are not alone in this life.

If you can find a path with no obstacles, it probably doesn't lead anywhere.

—FRANK A. CLARK

Overcoming Writer's Block

Remember the pencil I described in chapter one—the one with a razor-sharp point that will allow you to write anything your heart desires and a strong eraser that can transform your perceptions of many of your experiences? As you are holding this pencil in your hand, don't be surprised if you experience writer's block. Writer's block is a result of fears that can creep in when writing your story.

Many of us will have to confront writer's block on our journeys. These are behaviors that impede our growth and prevent us from putting the pencil to paper. It's those moments when it feels like time is running out, and we've yet to be productive or do something meaningful with our lives. This may cause us to feel tremendous guilt about how we've spent our time in the past or not knowing exactly how to move forward to create the future.

There can be many forms of writer's block, and with each person, they will vary. We will discuss three common blockages and what we can do to move past these barriers to discover the beauty in our stories. These common blockages are limiting beliefs, negative self-talk, and fear of failure/unknown.

Limiting Beliefs
Changing the Stories, You Tell Yourself

"Change the way you look at things and the things you look at will change."

—WAYNE DYER

Writer's block can come from many places—parents, family members, teachers, the media, and other community influences. They are views that keep us stuck and prevent us from believing in ourselves and our abilities. Below are examples of limiting beliefs—fill in the blanks:

I'll never be able to _____.
I'm too short (or tall) to _____.
I'm not _____ enough.
I know I'll fail because _____.
_____ will never accept me.

Do any of these sound familiar?

It is important that you pay attention to these limiting beliefs about yourself, others, or the world so you can be more intentional about telling yourself a different narrative, one that will propel you to create your masterpiece. Remember, you may not be able to change the past or events that have happened over the years; however, you can rewrite the meaning of what has taken place to provide yourself with a new narrative that will allow you to turn the page.

Because I was constantly preoccupied with negative thoughts, I've learned a few strategies that helped me to move outside my thoughts so I can enjoy the present moment. When I used to have negative thoughts about someone's behavior toward me or if I had a negative experience, I spent a lot of time and energy trying to figure out *why* this happened. These negative thoughts left me feeling stuck in the mud as if my wheels were spinning but my ride was going nowhere. For example, let's say I had been talking to a good friend every single day on the phone for the past few months and this friend didn't call for a couple of days. I would automatically assume something negative: maybe she didn't like me anymore, maybe she had found a replacement, or even worse, maybe I did or said something that got her upset. I would make up the worst scenarios, which made it difficult for me to concentrate on anything else. I would be so consumed with this perceived problem that I would spend a lot of time worrying, not being engaged in the present moment. Until I learned the art of telling myself a different story.

When you can tell yourself something different, you can move outside of trying to understand why something happened or didn't happen a lot faster. Instead of believing the worst, I would say something like maybe she's busy with her new job, or maybe she's spending more time with her new boyfriend. If the worrying doesn't go away, the best thing to do would be to pick up the phone and call my friend to check in. Not the type of check-in that would lead to me being critical of her not calling, but a genuine check-in to ensure she is well. The fact that I feel I must engage in a phone conversation with my friend every single day could reveal something deeper about my behavior. Maybe I'm too dependent or too needy. Telling yourself a more positive story will mean suspending past judgments and behaviors to create a new experience.

In *The Four Agreements: A Practical Guide to Personal Freedom*, author Don Miguel Ruiz says, "When you surrender and let go of the past, you allow yourself to be fully alive in the moment. Letting go of the past means you can enjoy the dream that is happening right now."[6]

Your turn! Go to the workbook and complete the exercise for Chapter 3: **BE** *Open.*

Negative Self-Talk

"*Convince yourself every day that you are worthy of a good life. Let go of stress, breathe. Stay positive, all is well.*"

—GERMANY KENT

Many of us go through life with two voices in our heads—a positive, upbeat, encouraging voice and a negative, fearful, and sometimes discouraging voice. We go about our day

---

6   "God is Life in Action," Goodreads, accessed April 1, 2020, https://www.goodreads.com/quotes/97787-god-is-life-god-is-life-in-action-the-best.

The Beauty Underneath the Struggle

not even realizing how these internal voices affect how we experience life.

Like limiting beliefs, this type of writer's block will have a mind of its own. It will show up no matter where you are. The goal is to not make it feel welcome. Limiting beliefs and negative self-talk go hand in hand, as the negative self-talk gives power and voice to our limiting beliefs. It's those things we say to ourselves that are harmful and that can prevent us from creating healthy relationships, taking new risks, or simply moving forward in a positive way.

For more than half of my life, I lived in the writing style of horror, a space of victimhood and guilt with no means of how to escape from the negative self-talk that filled my mind on a regular basis. Much of the emotional pain I felt, I attributed to my childhood. I was (and sometimes still am) a habitual thinker with unremitting negative self-talk. I didn't realize I could transform my inner dialogue into more caring and thoughtful conversations until a few years ago when I began to engage in new conversations with myself, which has led to more rewarding life experiences.

I have learned to have no regrets about my childhood or any of the blockages I've had in the past. I now realize that without those childhood experiences I deemed painful, I wouldn't have the passion, love, and dedication to do the work I am doing today. I wouldn't have the emotional or spiritual connection to write this book so that I can share my journey with you.

I believe everything happens for a reason. When we can tell ourselves a different story and change the conversations we have with ourselves, we can quickly advance to the next page of our life and resume writing a narrative of which we can be proud.

I've taken a few steps to challenge the negative self-talk in my head so that I could become free to experience life in a new way. These steps are as follows:

1. Acknowledge that there are two voices in your head, and it is your choice to listen to or to believe these thoughts.

2. Accept that the negative thought exist. Understanding that our thoughts can be negative will allow us to confront them as they show up. We can determine whether a thought is positive or negative by the way it makes us feel. If the thought is draining and fearful and brings about discouraging feelings, then it is probably negative. We can learn to notice our own self-talk as it happens and consciously choose to think about the situation in a way that brings us more peace, love, joy, and fulfillment.

The Beauty Underneath the Struggle

3. Question yourself. For several years I didn't question the negative voices that filled my head. Because I accepted this as my truth, they became my truth. Once I learned to question them like a lawyer or a judge, they became less powerful because they couldn't produce evidence to support their case. For instance, if there was a thought about someone not wanting me around, I would always ask myself, how do you know that is true? Did that person tell you this? Nine times out of ten, the responses to these questions would lead to *no evidence* because more than likely, I had not even talked to the person, which would have allowed them to explain their behavior. This leads to my last suggestion when dealing with negative self-talk.

4. Have courage. When negative self-talk pops into your head, have the courage not only to talk to yourself, but also to have a conversation with others if you feel the evidence is strong and it prevents you from moving forward.

Let's look at the example I used above in #3, question yourself: if for some reason you think that someone doesn't want to be around you and you have gathered evidence, such as the person leaving every time you arrive or never calling like they used to, find the courage to check in with the person, not to drill them about their behavior, but simply to state what you've observed and to ask if they are okay. Before doing this ask the following:

- Am I overreacting?
- What evidence do I have to support this?
- Are there other ways I can look at this?

You can transform negative self-talk today by challenging yourself with these questions every time you find yourself stuck in a negative thought.

And finally the last blockage we will discuss is...

Fear of Failure/Unknown

In *A Course in Miracles*, Marianne Williamson says:

Our deepest fear is not that we are inadequate. Our deepest fear is that we are powerful beyond measure. It is our light, not our darkness that most frightens us. We ask ourselves, "Who am I to be brilliant, gorgeous, talented, fabulous?" Actually, who are you not to be? You are a child of God. Your playing small does not serve the world.

The stories we tell ourselves and the negative self-talk give a platform for fear to take center stage. Fear arises when we feel threatened, and it alerts us to danger. The problem in most cases with fear is that, usually, there is nothing to be frightened of.

Being able to look at your past and rewrite the meaning of those experiences will not be easy; it will require a lot of courage. When you think of courage, you may think of having strength in the face of adversity. Courage is also a level of empowerment that many people may never experience in a lifetime, according to Dr. David R. Hawkins. Many of us are walking around asleep, unaware, and not courageous enough to accept that our story is a combination of the decisions we've made so far.

Following the five writing styles chart, which we discussed in chapter two, we reach rebirth/awakening (courage) when we no longer blame others or complain about the things in our lives that we don't like. It will take a lot of courage to accept responsibility for our current narrative. Once we accept that much of our lives is a result of our thoughts and actions/inactions, this empowerment will lead to growth and the boldness to grab the pencil and write our true desires. This is when you morph into the person you were meant to be because now that you are not reacting to the things around you,

you recognize your real superpower is your power to respond in a thoughtful way.

Clearing Past Blockages

When we are young, we relied on the adults in our lives to make choices for us. Many of us are unaware of our ability to write our own stories, as this authority has been overshadowed by what others want for us. Once we accept the fact that our life is the way it is due to our choices, we can own our life and circumstances and make different choices.

To create the story of your dreams, you will need to have the courage to make different choices, even when there's a chance that others will disagree with your decisions.

Picking up this book shows you are ready to be courageous and take action. You are in search of personal growth and want to become more aware of the thought patterns and behaviors keeping you from moving from where you are now to where you wish to be. George Addair described it best when he said, "Everything you've ever wanted is sitting on the other side of fear." Commit to yourself right now; commit to making it to the other side of fear.

Editing Your Perceptions

As you are determining your writing style, perception will play a huge part in the type of writer you will become.

The Beauty Underneath the Struggle

Perception is a mental representation of what is happening around us, although the picture we see is less about what is outside of us and more a reflection of what is inside.

One of our biggest downfalls as humans is that we don't realize how much we can actually control. We float from one place to another without intention, believing that life is happening *to* us instead of *for* us. We are the creators of our story, and it begins with our thoughts. Thoughts are powerful things—our thoughts create our own personal reality. We can use positive thoughts to create our own beautiful love story that we are eager to share with the world, or we can use our thoughts to create a horror story in which we suffer from feelings of guilt, shame, and despair. Will your writing style allow others/events to dictate your story or will you choose to write stories that will inspire others to share their stories? Which one will you choose?

Remember, change can and will happen, but it's going to take deliberate, intentional actions. Be mindful of shifting your perspective to look for the positives in life. When you do this, you will find lessons in the most negative, hopeless situations. When you look at a negative situation, layer a positive one on top of it. Visualize a better, more desirable outcome for the situation and hold this thought in your head. Those positive thoughts will attract more positive thoughts, your mood will shift, and you will have a much better story than the one you would have had if you had focused on negative events and allowed them to set the tone for your day, or even worse, your life.

Leaning into Failure to Create Possibilities

Failure Is an Option

The number one reason people avoid taking risks is the fear of failure. You can't avoid failure, nor should you want to. The idea is to have the courage to make a decision even when you are aware of the risks. Professors Emmanuel Manalo and Manu Kapur, of the learning sciences at the Swiss Federal Institute of Technology Zurich, compiled a research journal issue on the benefits of failure.[7] The issue's fifteen studies provide teachers and educational researchers with a guide for achieving success. One study concluded

---

[7] Emmanuel Manalo and Manu Kapur, *Thinking Skills and Creativity* 30 (December 2018).

that students do better when they fail. They were given complex tasks such as building a robot, and the students who failed at the task the soonest and most often actually did better than the other students. The idea is to take risks, fail, and learn from failure. So failure leads to more and often better possibilities. Once you understand that failure is a part of the journey, you will learn to lean into it to create more possibilities for your story.

I mentioned earlier that "everything happens for a reason." Sometimes, the reason we fail at something is to simply give us more possibilities or more opportunities. Abandon the idea that failure is final. View it as a doorway for more possibilities, which mean more experiences to gain the tools needed to create your best BUS story. Failure is never the end; it's the start of something new. Be grateful for it.

So now that we understand the benefits of failure and realize that failure is a necessary process, how do we lean into failure? How do we turn failures into success?

1. **Embrace the challenge.** Understand failure as a necessary part of your journey. You have not made the wrong decision. You are not defective if you fail. You have simply found a learning experience that will give you more information to write your story.

2. **Take responsibility**. Experience your rebirth/awakening. Adopt a writing style in which you take 100 percent responsibility for your life and actions. You are the author!

3. **Abandon the negative**. It is natural to experience momentary feelings that are less than upbeat after experiencing failure, but don't dwell on them. Remember, thoughts are things. If you continue to think negative thoughts, they will become your beliefs.

4. **Keep going**. There is no reason you should stop pursuing your goals because you experience failure. Do not use this as an excuse to abandon your dreams and goals. Regroup, plan, and keep pushing forward.

We are naturally drawn to experiences on the opposite end of the spectrum—the most positive and most negative experiences—and this forms our truth. This means we make current decisions based on past experiences that shape our belief system. Let's say, for example, as a child, you drive past a neighborhood of very nice homes. You don't know anyone who lives there, and when you ask your parents why your family doesn't live there, they tell you the homes are much too expensive, and no one they know lives there. This experience could form a belief system that money is scarce, and you will always lack the money to buy a home

The Beauty Underneath the Struggle

there. Fast forward to the future when you're searching for a home as an adult. You drive by that neighborhood, and you don't think to put any of the homes for sale there on your list. Because of the belief you've adopted, you may assume that these homes would be out of your price range because your perception of that neighborhood was created long before you were able to buy a home of your own. The opposite is also true. You could tell yourself a different story, one that creates more energy and encourages you to move outside of past beliefs to attach to new ones. You may see it as one of your goals to buy a home in that neighborhood, and because of this new belief or not accepting the old one, you and your family now reside in that neighborhood.

So long before we understand the ramifications, we begin to establish beliefs. Some serve us well, so we don't need to change them, but others begin to form a chain of limiting beliefs. Because of the risk of creating limiting beliefs that can block us from creating our BUS story, we should be mindful of the way we perceive the things that are happening around us. For example, you wake up and realize your child has missed the bus again. This means you will have to rush to get ready, grab breakfast, and take your child to school before heading to work. You decide as you're rushing around that this day is going to be terrible. Since you believe that, unfortunately, you're correct—you've set the tone for the day, and negative energy will likely follow you for the rest of the day, sending you spiraling further and further into negativity. But what happens if you choose not to give in to it? What if you choose to perceive things differently? You have the power to create a more positive outcome—a more positive day.

Your child has already missed the bus. The bus isn't coming back for him, and you know you will have to alter your day to get him to school. So instead of perceiving the morning events as negative, choose to find the positive. Maybe the extra time in the car with your child will give you time to talk to him about current events. Perhaps you can use the car time to give him a last-minute quiz for his upcoming spelling test. When you edit your perceptions, you edit your life.

Time Is Unstoppable: Value It!

Think about one of those important moments that has happened in your life—high school graduation, leaving home and going to college, marriage, or if you're like me, becoming a grandparent. There are so many things that happen in our lives, and when they do, we always ask, "Where did the time go?" How can we place a value on time, when it never stops moving? Take a glance at your watch or a clock right now, and already a lot of time has passed. And when you

The Beauty Underneath the Struggle

think about it, in just the few seconds it took to check the time, it didn't stop. Unbridled time is given to us the moment we enter the world. Time is both free and invaluable; once it's gone you cannot get it back.

When the average lifespan is seventy-nine years, why do we choose to waste so much of it?[8] At first glance, seventy-nine years seems like so much, but when you subtract the twenty-six years we spend sleeping and the years we spend working, how much time do we really have? It is less than we think. To live an intentional life is to be conscious of how we will spend every moment on this wonderful side of existence. To live an intentional life is to choose not to live a life deferred. You can recognize a life deferred by the thoughts and the words that are spoken. *When _____ happens, I'll pursue my passion. When I'm _____, I'll live the life I've always dreamed of. I'll find my purpose when _____.* As the saying goes, time waits for no man. It slips away unnoticed. You don't know it's gone until it's gone.

Those of us who are parents can attest to this truth. I remember when my girls were little babies, other parents would often say that I needed to enjoy these moments

---

[8] Chris Bailey, "Our Life Span Is Really Only 17.5 Years," A Life of Productivity, October 9, 2017, https://alifeofproductivity.com/our-life-span-is-only-17-5-years/.

because they grow up so quickly. "You'll blink," they would say, "and they grow up right before your eyes." Though I heard it time and time again, it did not mean much to me early on as I struggled through the night with feedings and lack of time for myself. I finally started to realize how true this was once my girls started kindergarten; it seemed like yesterday we were pushing a stroller and now they were growing more and more independent. Throughout your life you will experience milestones that influence the course of your story. Watching my girls go off to school was a milestone for all of us, and that milestone taught me an important lesson. Time had slipped through my hands, never to return. And now watching my daughter with her child, I can really see how important it is to value time. You can never get more time, but you can be intentional about how you plan to use your time moving forward.

Remember, you get to create your life. You are the only one who holds your pencil unless of course, you gift that privilege to someone else. Sometimes we forget we are in control of what we choose to focus on each day. We forget to listen to that inner voice that nudges us to do what we are called to do, the things that inspire us. Are you intentional about the way you spend your time? If not, how will you start to use the time you have to create more of what you desire?

The following daily practices will help you as you become more intentional with time:

1. **Protect your time.** Abandon the need to say yes when you want to say no. Saying yes to things you don't want to do takes time away from the things that bring you great purpose.

2. **Practice gratitude.** Before closing your eyes at night and upon waking in the morning, visualize five things you are thankful for. Keep a grateful journal and reflect and add to it often.

3. **Breathe**. Take time out each day to remind yourself to take deep, clean breaths for twenty seconds or more. My Apple Watch reminds me to do this, but you can set reminders on your phone or make it a habit to breathe at routine times, such as right before your lunch break, so you don't forget.

4. **Exercise.** Fit in some form of exercise at least three times per week. Not only is it good for the body, it's also good for mind and spirit.

5. **Unplug.** Resist the urge to spend most of your time or all of your free time mindlessly scrolling through social media, answering text messages, or reading emails. Unplug for part of the day.

6. **Practice kindness.** Kindness goes a long way. Find at least one way to say or do something nice for someone you come in contact with. It can be as simple as paying a stranger a compliment.

7. **Learn something new.** Whether it be talking with another person, reading a book, or listening to a podcast, make it a habit to learn something new every day.

Practicing these habits daily will help you become more intentional with your time so that you're not stumbling through life on autopilot.

If this feels too overwhelming, choose one or two from the list to start, master the one or two you've selected, and then add on another until you fully implement all seven tasks into your daily routine. The one you start with will depend on you. My advice is to choose the one you know you would struggle with the most. If you can conquer that one, the rest will easily fall into place.

For me, I struggled with the need to always say yes. People would ask me for my help, to attend events, or for random favors, and I would always say yes. It felt natural to do so, and the rare occasions I said no, I would feel guilty about it for weeks. This resulted in me constantly feeling overwhelmed, unappreciated, and overworked. I would

The Beauty Underneath the Struggle

then zone out and stumble through life on autopilot, just to get through each day.

This was not the way I wanted to live. This was not a good way to share my gift with the world and release the fire I had within.

What will implementing at least one of these tasks into your daily life do for you? How would it change your life?

Commit to change now!

4

BE Courageous

"Courage isn't having the strength to go on—
it is going on when you don't have strength."
—NAPOLEON BONAPARTE

Have Courage

A couple of months ago, I was led once again to do something that made me feel a little uncomfortable- organize family Bible Study. Our weekly Bible studies have turned out to be a wonderful opportunity to spend time with loved ones, especially since no one can travel and see one other during the pandemic. These moments have given us a chance to reconnect in a spiritual way and have been a blessing to our lives.

Each session is led by a different family member, and each time, I've walked away with new insight that adds value to this book. As I wrote this section on courage, my Aunt Francis led our Bible study and read a passage from Dr. Martin Luther King Jr.'s book, *Stride Toward Freedom*.[9] I thought this passage would be great to share here, as Dr. King's life has been a model of overcoming fear to embrace courage.

During his lifetime, when there was much to be fearful of, King demonstrated tremendous courage. He was often attacked by white supremacist groups and even members of his own race, but King relied heavily on love and his faith in God. He acted despite uncertainty. Like King, we all struggle with fear, and the only way to combat our fears is through great courage.

One such example of King's courage is described in his book *Stride toward Freedom*.[10]

In chapter eight, King describes a time in which he and his wife, Coretta, were receiving threatening phone calls. King states in his book:

Almost every night I went to bed faced with uncertainty of the next moment. In the morning I would

---

[9] Martin Luther King Jr., *Stride toward Freedom* (Boston: Beacon Press, 2010), 124–126.

[10] King Jr., *Stride toward Freedom*, 124–126.

The Beauty Underneath the Struggle

look at Coretta and "Yoki" and say to myself: "They can be taken away from me at any moment; I can be taken away from them at any moment." For once I did not even share my thoughts with Coretta.

One night toward the end of January I settled into bed late, after a strenuous day. Coretta had already fallen asleep and just as I was about to doze off the telephone rang. And an angry voice said, "Listen, nigger, we've taken all we want from you; before next week you'll be sorry you ever came to Montgomery." I hung up, but I couldn't sleep. It seemed that all my fears had come down on me at once. I had reached the saturation point.

I got out of bed and began to walk the floor. Finally, I went to the kitchen and heated a pot of coffee. I was ready to give up. With my cup of coffee sitting untouched before me I tried to think of a way to move out of the picture without appearing a coward. In this state of exhaustion, when my courage had all but gone, I decided to take my problem to God. With my head in my hands, I bowed over the kitchen table and prayed aloud... at that moment I experienced the presence of the Divine as I had never experienced Him before. It appears I could hear the quiet assurance of an inner voice saying: "Stand up for righteousness, stand up

for the truth; and God will be at your side forever."
Almost at once, my fears began to go. My uncertainty disappeared. I was ready to face anything.

A few nights later, Dr. King's home was bombed while his wife and baby were home alone. King was attending a mass meeting at a church. King says that the news of the bombing didn't rattle him, as the experience he had with God a few nights before had given him courage. He said to the attendees at the meeting, "Let us keep moving...with faith that what we are doing is right, and with the even greater faith that God is with us in the struggle."

Like Dr. King, we will all have our fears. The goal is to continue moving in the face of adversity.

When you believe in something bigger than yourself, you realize that you are not the sum of your limitations and you open the door for miracles to take place.

When we think of Dr. King or other well-known personalities we see on television or in the movies, we may assume that they don't have fears. We watch in awe as they share their gifts and only wish we had the courage to do the same. Adele (the singer) openly admits that she's scared of audiences. Emma Watson, who plays Hermione Granger in the Harry Potter movies, says she suffers from stage fright on occasions, and the list of people with fears goes on and on. But the one thing these people have in common is the courage to push through their fears and to take action despite uncertainty.

We can all do great things, but sometimes we allow our fears to step in and paralyze our ability to move forward. Fear of failure, fear of the unknown, even fear of success tends to create those negative *what if* stories that can prevent us from writing and living the life we desire. Our minds play out undesirable outcomes in which things go wrong, like a movie, and these thoughts tend to spiral into writing the narrative of every bad thing that could possibly happen, which will then prevent us from ever taking the first step.

So to live out our best BUS stories, we must have courage. Courage is having the ability to focus on the possibilities instead of the mishaps. It's encouraging yourself to take the risk by transforming your *what if something goes wrong* beliefs into *what if something goes right*? Changing the *what if* stories to include a positive outcome by asking yourself "what if things go well?" will compel you to create a story of success, giving you the energy to go through with the task.

*Take a moment and go to your workbook and complete the exercise for Chapter 4: **BE** Courageous ~ "Transforming What If Stories."*

Take Action

> *Doubt, of whatever kind, can be ended by action alone.*
>
> —Thomas Carlyle

Isaac Newton's first law states that every object will remain at rest or in uniform motion in a straight line unless compelled to change its state by the action of an external force. Simply put, if you don't do anything, you will remain exactly where you are. If you don't take action to change your story, your story will not change. Most of us understand this on a fundamental level, yet when it comes to rewriting our story and taking action, we falter. Why? Quite often, uncertainty is the culprit. It's difficult to take chances, open ourselves to risk, and step outside our comfort zones. It's easy to remain exactly where we are, do the things we're accustomed to, and allow the same characters to remain in our story—even when it does not serve us.

Beware of procrastination disguised as action. Sometimes we read a piece of motivational material, listen to an uplifting podcast, or attend a self-improvement seminar and walk away feeling inspired to take action. However, feelings are fleeting; if you don't act on the information you glean from outside sources, it loses its effectiveness. It rolls

The Beauty Underneath the Struggle

around in your head, gets you pumped, and makes you feel good for a short period of time—which has its benefits—but it does nothing to change your story in the long term if you choose not to put what you learned in action. Remember the introduction of this book, when I asked you to pledge to not only keep an open mind during this journey but also to take action? Look back at your workbook and the actions you've taken since making that promise. Have you actually done anything with the new learning thus far? If not, pause for a moment and commit to change now.

If you find yourself walking in fear and uncertainty and refusing to enter situations unless you know exactly how they will turn out, it will stop you from taking action and doing something new. Neil Gaiman, a British writer who earned critical praise and popular success with richly imagined fantasy tales, compared writing to driving through fog when he said, "You can't really see where you're going. You have just enough of the road in front of you to know that you're probably still on the road, and if you drive slowly and keep your headlamps lowered, you'll still get where you were going." The same is true when you're writing your BUS story. There will be times when you take a step in a certain direction, but you can only see one foot ahead of you. That may seem intimidating, but pursue it anyway. When you take that step, the next one will appear. Commit to changing the need to have every piece of the puzzle before taking the first step. Commit to change now.

When I left my position as principal to start my own business, I had a vision, but I couldn't see each step in advance. Because of all the signs that preceded me leaving, I made the decision and took a leap of faith. I often refer to the experience as building a plane that had already taken off. The road to take and the characters to add all unfolded along the way. If I hadn't taken that one step to leave a career I loved, to start a business I love, my dream would have died. Now, I'm not advocating that you quit your job on a whim, but I am advocating that you refuse to walk in fear, put your ear to your heart to listen to your dreams, and take action. Commit to change now.

Casting Call: Positive Characters Wanted!

Being selective about the characters you choose for your story deserves its own section. When motivational speaker Jim Rohn said, "You're the average of the five people you spend the most time with," it resonated with many. Why? Because it's true, and for the most part, it's easily measurable. Take a look around at the five people you speak with, hang out with, or do business with the most. Make a mental note of their beliefs, both good and bad, their habits, their income level, the vacations they go on, their failures,

The Beauty Underneath the Struggle

and their successes. Now, think about your own. You will likely fall somewhere in the middle, or the average, of the five people you spend your time with. That in itself is not necessarily problematic, but when you seek to transform your life, it sure can be. If you seek to create your BUS story and live a positive life, yet you spend the majority of your time around people with low-level energy, who are the polar opposite of what you want, every effort toward your transformation will be challenging.

My mother had two sayings she would say quite often when encountering negative people: "birds of a feather flock together" and "misery loves company." I'm sure you have heard these sayings, or you may even use them yourself. Though cliché in modern society, these sayings are rooted in fact. They are based on universal laws that govern the universe. These sayings, specifically, are based on the law of vibration. The law of vibration, commonly stated and understood as "like attracts like," tells us that nothing rests, everything moves, everything vibrates. We don't commonly think of ourselves as energy, but that's exactly what we are. Just as the chair you are sitting in or the floor you walk on is energy, so are you. You are just vibrating on a different frequency.

Therefore, selecting the characters for your story should take some time. Think about the film industry. Rarely, if ever, are characters cast in a role with little to no research. There is a process. When a role is announced, there are submissions from agents (the gatekeepers). Headshots, résumés, and videos are analyzed, and finally, there are auditions. The process is even more stringent when the main character is selected. In our personal lives, the process of selecting whom we choose to occupy our space may not be as rigorous, but we should still have standards. Once people are allowed in our lives, we should check to see if they should remain there.

I'm sure you have two questions right now: How do I choose more positive characters for my story? If I want to improve myself, does that mean I have to cut off people who are not where I want to be in life? Let's tackle the first question. As you write your story, own your awesomeness, and radiate success, the same type of people will be drawn to you. They will be attracted to your story, your mission, and your success. We are all made up of energy, and like attracts like. Think of it like a radio frequency. When you are on a higher frequency, there will be nothing but positivity, mindfulness, kindness, and success. Those who seek what you seek in life will easily find your frequency. They will be drawn to it. The opposite is also true. Those who do not share your desire for positivity will be repelled by your frequency, opting to stay on a lower frequency until they are ready to see the same type of growth in their lives. This eliminates the need to cut people off most of the time; they will usually cut themselves off. Then some people will surprisingly rise to your energy level, and this is always a good thing.

So what do you do when the negativity comes from your own family or coworkers? This can be challenging, especially when the negative energy comes from people with whom you must engage with often. I had to convince myself that it was okay to spend less time with negative people, even when they were in my own family or work situations. Think about it—it's enough having to fight with your own thoughts and negative beliefs, but when it's compounded with others' negative attitudes and beliefs about you or even themselves, it can prevent you from moving forward and taking the risks necessary to become the person you were intended to be. In other words, it makes it more challenging for you to take risks and become the hero of your story when you are constantly hanging out with the villains. So give yourself permission to let go of or spend less time with people whose energy will not propel you to move forward.

Go to your workbook and complete the exercise for Chapter 4: **BE** *Courageous ~ "Surround Yourself with Positive People."*

Casting the Right People for the Right Roles

My husband left his job with the school district in July 2019 to join me on this amazing journey. Kermit is no longer just my life partner; he is my business partner, hand chosen not just because of his personal relationship with me, but also because of his ability to support and cheer me on. I mention this because we often position people in our lives to take on more roles than they're qualified for because it feels comfortable, and this can lead to disaster. I've seen the same practices performed in schools and other organizations. We place people in positions because they've been in the organization for a while and we feel a sense of obligation to either give them the job or the promotion despite their ability to perform. This is not good practice, nor will it help to move the organization toward success.

Kermit and I, gratefully, are the average of each other. Now more than four years later, we have a thriving business with ten other amazing people who work with us and who share our passion for transforming culture. Working alongside each other naturally means we spend a good portion of our day together. The people we chose to be a part of our team were selected not only for their ability to work alongside me to propel our company forward, but also for the positive contributions that they could make to the company's overall story. My story is now their story and theirs mine. These are people who not only believe in our vision of transforming schools, but also have the skills to make our vision a reality.

What we do repeatedly will become a habit. Speaking with the same types of people, on the same types of subjects, may not advance your story. You will most likely become complacent. Had I not been selective with the people I surround myself with, my business idea would not have evolved. So as you're selecting the characters for your story, always remember "the choice is yours."

Focus on Something Bigger Than Yourself

#OneChance

"I have my good days and my bad days. Today is a good day." That's the way Tish answered the phone when I called to interview her.

I recently spoke to my cousin, Latissue Colbert, who lost her son Chance, at nineteen years old, to gun violence on July 21, 2019. I wanted to speak with Tish because her and Chance's story had inspired me and so many. Although we had not talked in several years and I had never met Chance, I felt so connected with her family during this time as I took part in the comments, celebrations of Chance's life, and memories that were shared on social media. I was happy to reconnect with Tish and excited for her to be a part of my story.

I didn't have any questions prepared for Tish, and it seemed I didn't need to: my cousin jumped in right away and began sharing stories about Chance and the lives he had touched during his nineteen years on this earth. She said there were so many young people at Chance's home-going that she didn't even know. A few of them expressed that Chance had given them a ride once, and others simply expressed how he had helped them out in some way.

These included young people he would observe sitting alone at lunch and would stop to sit with; two freshman boys he mentored during his senior year; and members of Students of Suicide (SOS), a suicide prevention program, where he learned more about suicide and how to identify peers who might be suicidal. He even visited different schools to talk about the risks. It seemed that the same spirit Tish had poured into Chance, he had poured into others.

I admired Tish's resiliency as she told me she returned to work a week after Chance's funeral. She said that she's not one to go into the house, close the door, and eat and drink her life away. Doing so would result

The Beauty Underneath the Struggle

in all the hard work and encouragement she had given to Chance going down the drain. She would often tell Chance, "God's got this!" Chance loved football, and she encouraged him to be an asset both on and off the field and pushed him always to be his best! And now the same encouraging words she used to say to Chance, she says to herself.

She told me that all of who she is, is because of God and that all the experiences she's had in her life make her very different from others, and she accepts this gift that God has given her.

In the few years before Chance passed, Tish was faced with many other struggles—her house caught fire, her brother was diagnosed with prostate cancer, her father became very ill, and both her thirteen-year-old nephew and her uncle passed away.

When I asked Tish what advice she would give to others who have lost their loved ones, she said, "You know when people tell you that God will give you strength? Well, he really does. Everyone has an expiration date. God has a plan for each of us, and while we are here, we need to love on each other more and be positive because death is inevitable; it's going to happen. Would I have done more to shelter him? No, I wouldn't. I allowed him to *live*! And so, I have no regrets. You only get #OneChance."

Tish and her son, Chance

When you wake up each day, knowing that there is a greater power at work in your life, you feel a sense of confidence and purpose. Your belief could be in love, kindness, faith, or courage; whatever it is, this knowing will give you the energy to move forward even when you lack the energy to take a step.

When my girls were young, before dropping them off at school, we would make it a habit to pray before they got out of the car. All the fear, doubt, and uncertainty would fade away as they stepped out of the car to begin their journey.

Knowing that what was in store for them once they exited the car was beyond my control, my faith gave me the courage to live my day as if they would be taken care of.

There will be times when we are in the midst of struggles and we just don't want to do it. We want to give up, and we can't see the sliver of light in the darkness. That is when we need to stop and ask ourselves why we do what we do. If your purpose for life is only found in you, you are sure to fail. Before every event, I always pray that God will use me for his will and to remind me that it's not about me and all about him! This simple prayer is a reminder that what I do is bigger and greater than me.

We were not put on this earth to serve ourselves. We're here to use our lives, our stories, to make the world a better place and to make a contribution to the lives of others. When we truly understand that living for something bigger than ourselves can have a huge impact on the world, that is when we realize our lives are not just about us. Like Tish said, "We all come with an expiration date." We're not going to be around forever, so we should become part of something that will. Decide to be someone who inspires others. As Gandhi said, "The best way to find yourself is to lose yourself in the service of others."

When you live for something bigger than yourself, your impact becomes greater. While doing so, you will realize that your mission is so much bigger than yourself. You'll also be driven to push the limits to realize fully how far you can go. Take my story as an example: I once aspired to work in a school serving as a teacher. I later aspired to serve as a principal. Once I understood the impact I could have on students and teachers in one school, I realized that I could go even bigger! I could reach students and teachers in multiple schools with my message. When you focus on something bigger than yourself, you will attract people who share the same desire. Together, you will achieve something greater than you ever envisioned. You will understand the importance of giving back to others, and in the process, you will discover things about yourself you never knew: the things that empower you, the things that you want to fight for, the things you truly find important. You will become happier because now you understand your purpose, and your life will have greater meaning.

It's easy to get out of bed in the morning when you understand your mission and what you were sent here to do. You'll wake up with the fire of wanting to go to work rather than having to go to work! And nothing and nobody can stop you when you have that type of fire inside. You will stand up to trials and adversity, and you will learn how to fight to achieve your goals instead of giving up and giving in. You can then use that knowledge for other areas in your

The Beauty Underneath the Struggle

life or to give lessons to others who are struggling with how to work through a problem. Do you see how it all comes full circle? This is what focusing on something bigger than yourself does. Leave your mark on the world. Think big and keep pushing forward.

Commit to change now!

5

BE Grateful

"Acknowledging the good that you already have in your life is the foundation for all abundance."

—ECKHART TOLLE

The Power of Gratitude

Gratitude is the manifestation of joy, commitment, and devotion toward those who are meaningful to us. It encompasses shared experiences, love, and understanding that the universe has conspired to connect all of us for the good of mankind.

Often, gratitude and thankfulness are used interchangeably to express appreciation for something or someone, but when you really think about it, these two words are in a class of their own. Allow me to explain.

Nine times out of ten, you've already said thank you to someone today.

I had a dentist appointment the other day, and after thanking God for waking me up, thanking Kermit for dropping me off, and thanking the dentist office staff, I was pretty sure I had said the words *thank you* more than fifteen times (and that doesn't even count me thanking my daughter Brooklynn for loading the dishwasher). We will probably say or hear *thank you* a lot in one day.

Being thankful is in the same family as the phrases "yes ma'am," "no sir," "please," and "excuse me." There are automatic sayings we were taught during family belief camp as a show of respect, especially toward the adult figures in our lives.

When I was a child, if you didn't respond in this way when told to do something or when someone did something nice for you, this would be seen as a sign of disrespect. Being thankful is usually rooted in what is happening at the moment: we say *thank you* when someone compliments us or when we receive a gift on our birthday; however, these feelings of being thankful are usually short-lived.

When thinking about the two words, I, too, have been guilty of using them in the same context, but when we look at them more closely, we see that being grateful is the result of showing or giving thanks. *Merriam-Webster's Dictionary* defines *thankful* as "conscious of benefits received." It is a conscious act from the person who received the benefits. Little babies learn this very early. Think about it. If a baby drops his toy on the floor, and someone picks it up and hands it back to the child, how will the parent usually respond? The parent will probably say, "So what do you say?" already training their little one to repeat these automatic responses.

Saying thank you has become an instant habit right after someone does something for us, like opening the door, handing us the remote control to the television, or getting us a glass of water: we usually seal the deal with *thank you*.

However, when we look at the word *grateful*, it's a little more divine in nature. *Merriam-Webster's Dictionary* defines being grateful as being "appreciative of benefits received." While I believe this is true, the term *appreciation* doesn't give the word *grateful* the acknowledgment it deserves, as being grateful is not so easy to achieve.

Gratefulness is in the same family as joy, as it's a spirit that doesn't need a smile, and you can experience it in the deepest moment of struggle. Being thankful may not show up in darkness and struggle, whereas gratefulness never leaves; like joy, it is always present inside us as an untapped reservoir.

It is the pure spirit of being at peace with one's self and the world. Experiencing gratitude is the same as experiencing God. It's not a quick thing you say out of habit in the

101

check-out line when the cashier hands you your receipt. Gratitude comes from the heart, whereas thankfulness can come from the head.

If we refer to our writer's style chart in chapter two, the love story encompasses a level of gratitude, as this is a level of unconditional love for self and others where there is no judgment. When we work hard to give thanks for every moment, gratitude becomes our reward.

So Give Thanks

"Thankfulness is the beginning of gratitude. Gratitude is the completion of thankfulness. Thankfulness may consist merely of words. Gratitude is shown in acts."
—HENRI-FRÉDÉRIC AMIEL

Every morning I wake up and my feet hit the floor, I give thanks to God for another day. The power of gratitude cannot be underestimated. It is the power to transform a negative experience into a positive one. I've learned to be thankful for all of my experiences, both the good and those I perceive as bad, which have given me the strength and energy to keep writing and refining my story. I know that these small acts of being thankful will lead me to feel more grateful in each moment.

The Beauty Underneath the Struggle

People who have created their BUS stories understand this truth, and among other things, this has become an important part of their thinking habits. Gratitude is an emotion of thankfulness and appreciation, and this leads to a life of mindfulness and contentment. Instead of tuning out the present and fixating on the next event, feeling, or achievement, gratefulness stills the mind and anchors us in the present moment. If we don't practice being grateful we can suffer feelings of lack and insufficiency. Especially in the age of social media, it is common for us, who have so much to feel grateful for, to feel inadequate instead because we are constantly comparing our lives to the highlight reels of others. We forget to take notice of all the things we have to be thankful for, which can cause us to slip into writing horror stories, the lowest level writing style. When we are thankful for all that we have—the good and the bad, the lessons and achievements—we experience gratitude. Practicing being in the moment will help to shift your thinking from the negative to the positive. Let's face it, you cannot delegate the job to someone else and seek fulfillment through the actions of others; it has to come from within.

When Kermit and I first got married, he would often ask me what he could do to make me happy. One day I finally said to him, "If you want to make me happy, be happy!" As I stated in chapter three, our energy is contagious, and if

103

we want to attract more positive things into our lives, we need to be mindful of how we are showing up. In other words, I just wanted Kermit to be thankful and happy in the moment because I knew his energy would influence my energy.

Many times, our environment can be a barometer of our level of gratefulness and appreciation for life. Look around right now at the room you're sitting in, the car you're driving, your children, your spouse/significant other. Pause and take it all in. If the things around you are not bringing some sense of joy and fulfillment, this could possibly be an indication of your inability to experience gratitude.

Before moving to the next section, take one minute and give thanks for all you have.

Either do this silently now or go to Chapter 5: **BE** Grateful~ *The Power of Gratitude"* in your workbook and jot them down.

Take note of how you feel after taking a moment to give thanks. In our fast-paced society, it's important to take time (if only a minute) each day to give thanks, as it's easy for

The Beauty Underneath the Struggle

gratitude to fall by the wayside, but remember it's always there, and we only need to tap into it.

It's easy to be thankful when we get that promotion, new job, house, or good news from a doctor's visit, but all these things are temporary, and we often find ourselves searching for the next quick fix or the next thing to make us happy. It's a never-ending dash through life to get to some fabricated destination, but we are missing out on the beauty of the journey. Take time each day to reflect on all you have and all you went through to accomplish it. You've worked hard, so be grateful. That's not to say you shouldn't create more goals; rather, it is to remind you to take a moment and enjoy the here and now!

My desire for you is that you can release the negative energy from the day before and think only of all the things you have, instead of what you don't have. Once you become consistent in taking time to give thanks, you will find that you will feel a sense of joy permeate through every part of your body, mind, and spirit. When you start your morning being thankful, you will attract more positive energy throughout your day. Your mood will be improved because you cannot hold positive thoughts in a negative mind. You will find that as you move through your day, your thankful mindset will lead to what we all desire: a grateful heart.

"As we express our gratitude, we must never forget that the highest appreciation is not to utter words, but to live by them."

—JOHN F. KENNEDY

Ready to grow in gratitude? The following are just a few things you can do to focus more on the things that bring you joy:

1. **First, focus on your level of consciousness and practice mindfulness**. By staying in the present moment, you will find that there is really nothing happening. When you learn to calm your mind from manipulating thoughts, you will find more space to connect with spirit.

2. **Make time** each day to create and repeat positive affirmations which will help you overcome limiting beliefs about yourself, others, and the world. Some examples are *I am smart*, *I am kind*, and *I am thankful* for the universe and the blessings it holds.

3. **Keep a gratitude journal!** Tim Ferriss, a successful entrepreneur and author of *The 4-Hour Workweek*, says he takes five minutes each morning to write down what he's grateful for and what he's looking forward to because it "allows [him] to not only get

more done during the day but to also feel better throughout the entire day, to be a happier person, to be a more content person." Journaling improves your mood because you are forced to enter into reflection. This sends you from a negative space to a positive one. Use a journal, a special tablet, or even a sheet of paper and just write! Write down everything you're grateful for: your health, car, house, family, friends, et cetera. List it all, feel the feeling of gratitude, and watch your energy soar! When you feel grateful for what you have, you attract more of what you love.

And finally...

4. **Share positive messages on social media!** I love posting inspirational messages on both my business and personal social media platforms. Everyone could use a little positive energy, and why not share it with your friends and family?

Which brings me to showing gratitude toward others.

Gratitude is not a gift that should be bottled up and kept to yourself but manifested and shared with others. The magic of gratitude is that it can extend from you, your household, or your job to the entire world. In his book *Power vs. Force*, Dr. David R. Hawkins reveals that "one individual who lives and vibrates to the energy of pure love and reverence for all of life will counterbalance the negativity of 750,000 individuals who calibrate at the lower weakening levels"[11] This means by regularly showing gratitude toward others, we can dramatically improve our world for the good of all.

When you wake up in the morning and your spouse has your cup of coffee ready for you or has heated your car for you, take a moment to stop and give thanks! Be thankful that you have someone who looks out for you, someone who cares about the little things that make your day go well. Express that gratitude by saying, "I really appreciate you taking the time to make coffee for me. That really means a lot." Watch the joy and energy you radiate spread to that person, and more than likely he or she will share that gratitude with someone else.

The next time you're at dinner, stop and savor the flavors. You can enjoy a meal prepared by someone else, who may use cooking to express his or her special gift. If you enjoy the meal, express your gratitude to the cook. Your gratitude just may inspire that person to continue sharing the special gift of cooking with the world. When your children speak to you, really listen to them. Focus on what they're saying and repeat what they have said to you. Take a moment to appreciate that conversation.

---

[11] Hawkins, *Power vs. Force*, 112.

Gratitude in *Moments of Struggle*

As I stated earlier, being grateful is akin to having joy, as it's a spirit that doesn't need a smile and you can experience it in the deepest moment of struggle. Thankfulness may not show up in darkness and struggle, but you can always count on gratefulness to be there; like joy, it is always present inside us as an untapped reservoir.

It's probably hard to imagine being grateful in times of struggle because when we're in the middle of a challenge, we are so focused on the problem or the things that are not right that we can't see the road in front of us. Sometimes when we're in it, we feel doomed, as if the sun will never rise again. These times, more than ever, are the times we must provide ourselves with a big dose of gratitude and remind ourselves of all the blessings around us. We must also remember that "this too shall pass," just like every other challenge we've faced: if we live through it, we will get through it. It brings great comfort when you remember to be grateful while in the struggle. Let me share with you a few strategies that have helped me find the beauty while I'm in the struggle.

- **Be Your *Best* Coach!**
  Learn to talk back to the thoughts that have you trapped in a horror story with feelings of being a

victim. Coach yourself up by having a go-to mantra that will help you to rise above the current situation. Some of my best coaching tips for myself are: "This too shall pass;" "It's not about you;" and my favorite, "Hasn't God brought you through before? What makes you think He won't do it again?"

- **Focus on the Positive.**

  When you're faced with a challenging situation, it may be hard to focus on the positive. This is a good time to put the power of gratitude into action! Pause, look around, and instead of focusing on the things that are not going well, focus on the things that are. Give yourself time for those things to soak into your spirit and enjoy the moment. And finally...

- **Do Something for Someone Else**

  Remember, you were created to serve. You were not put on this earth to think only of yourself and your problems. When my girls were younger, like me, they often struggled with negative thinking. When their energy levels were low and they descended into a victim mindset (horror story), I would always encourage them to go and do something for someone else. Service to others heals the human spirit and gives way for your light to shine while bringing joy to others.

Experience the *Joy* of Learning

Don't be surprised if you walk into his classroom and you find him standing on top of a desk or students celebrating their accomplishments to the sound of music and sights of a shiny, groovy disco ball!

Meet Shaughn Thomas, a middle school teacher and founder of Invest in Yourself, an after-school program that focuses on financial literacy. Shaughn's teaching style is dynamic and innovative to say the least, and his goal is to provide students with an adventurous learning experience. Shaughn will tell you that he gets just as much joy from teaching as students do from learning because he considers himself a student first.

His career didn't start in education; as a matter of fact, education was a second career for him. So he hasn't always been surrounded by other educators who appreciate his innovative style of teaching; in fact, there have been a few educators on his journey who have tried to convince him to take the traditional route to teaching and those who have told him that his style will not work. Shaughn states that when people tell him he can't do or accomplish something, he's even more motivated to prove otherwise.

Because Shaughn expresses a spirit of gratitude, this same level of appreciation is evident in the way his students respond to his instruction—again, the energy you put into life is the energy you will get back. Shaughn makes sure that he not only shows up, but shows out, and his positive attitude is reflected in the positive way students respond to his teaching style. Shaughn's courage and willingness to follow his passion have earned him many rewards, and he has been featured in several newspapers, magazines, and news shows. Shaughn's purpose allows him to live in the moment and enjoy learning while creating a life that inspires others to do the same.

Shaughn Thomas

Learning Doesn't Just Happen in the Classroom

"Learning is the only thing the mind never exhausts, never fears, and never regrets."

—LEONARDO DA VINCI

When people think of learning, often they think of a classroom setting, whether it be K–12 or college. While these early academic experiences are an important part of our journey, learning does not start the moment you enter school, and it certainly doesn't stop when you walk across the stage at graduation. In life, learning never stops. Self-awareness is a form of learning that can inspire you to make the change necessary to live an inspired life. You are continually collecting data through experiences on a day-to-day basis. There are lessons to be learned, challenges sent to push you to your limit, and experiences that provide tools for your toolbox. The key is to find joy throughout the process, no matter how difficult the lesson. Be grateful for the lessons.

You will go through tough experiences to gain new learning and acquire a new appreciation for life. Though it may be difficult to accept that this negative experience is for the highest good of all involved, learn to be grateful for the experience and accept it. When I was principal and was told I had to discontinue using principles that had proven so beneficial to our school, it stung a little at first, but I am grateful for the lesson! It wasn't the principles that had actually transformed our culture; our culture was a reflection of effectively communicating our values and goals. Now I travel the country, helping other school leaders to create common practices and goals for their school. This would probably have never been possible if not for the struggle I faced.

Learning should be a lifelong, continual process. Albert Einstein once said, "Once you stop learning, you start dying." When you embrace lessons in your life and eagerly seek them out, learning is part of your journey to writing your BUS story. Embrace learning and find the joy in it. Explore your interests and commit to learning everything you can about them. Here is where special gifts are uncovered. When you make learning an integral part of your life, others will be drawn to you for your ability to share the lessons you have learned.

When I conduct trainings/workshops, superintendents and other district leaders will often stop in to observe. While conducting a workshop in my home state, I met a superintendent who actually sat at the table with a group of teachers and stayed the duration of the meeting, participating in the activities and joining in the discussions. I watched him throughout the training as he moved around from table to table, chatting with everyone in the room. I noticed that he talked and smiled but mostly listened, nodded, and asked probing questions as a way to engage and learn from others. The people gathered at the tables seemed to enjoy having him visit and didn't treat him as a superior at all as they casually tapped him on the shoulders, gave him high fives, and shared pictures of their families. At first, I chalked up his likability to charisma and charm, but by the end of the training, I mustered up the courage to ask him what brings him so much joy. I still remember his response today. "Learning," he said. "Learning keeps me young; as long as there's something more for me to learn, the more days I will have to stay here to learn it." People who find joy in learning are usually intrinsically motivated and engaged, which can lead to a long life!

When you allow knowledge to liberate you, you will react to circumstances based on fact (knowledge) instead of from a place of ignorance. Negative thoughts and low-level energy often come from a lack of awareness. Some get stuck in a horror story because they lack the knowledge to free themselves. In *The Power of Intention*, Dr. Wayne Dyer tells us, "Low-level energy people cannot distinguish truth from falsehood. They can be told how to think, whom to hate, whom to kill; and they can be herded into a group-think mentality based on such trivial details as what side of the river they were born on, what their parents and their grandparents believed, the shape of their eyes, and hundreds of other factors having to do with appearance and total identification with their material world."[12]

When you expand your knowledge through life lessons, you will continue to propel your life forward instead of remaining stagnant. Being on autopilot and completing tasks without questioning why you're completing them will prevent you from expanding your mindset and creating new experiences. Your mind yearns to solve problems. If you don't give it the right problems to solve, it will go in search of its own challenges. We are wired constantly to absorb information and to do something with that information. Never stop learning. Find freedom and joy in the lessons of life, no matter how difficult, and use them to enrich the lives of others as part of your legacy.

Embracing New Beliefs

By now you have learned to identify your core beliefs. You have learned that *you* need to be the author of your story by taking responsibility for your story. You have examined

---

[12] Wayne Dyer, *The Power of Intention* (Carlsbad: Hay House, 2004), 111.

The Beauty Underneath the Struggle

your purpose and learned to believe in yourself by embracing choice. You've also learned how to find the courage to live out your story. You have created new beliefs that will help you thrive. I'm proud of you, reader, for taking the steps to learn what it takes to rewrite your story. You're awesome! You're the best! You rock!

But now for a moment of truth. You have to *act* your way into a new belief system. Only when you transfer the beliefs from your mind into physical reality will you have truly embraced change. When you take action in the external world, you will see a new reality form outside of you. That new reality is reflected back to you through experiences and becomes a new thought or belief system reflected back to you. You have got to embrace the things you have learned in this book as your new beliefs in order to see change. That's going to be the only way to ensure you continue on your path.

Listen, there will be days when the old you and beliefs threaten to resurface. The body and the mind seek balance, and after you go through a period of new inspiration, your body and mind will threaten to fall back into what you've fed it the longest. There will be family members or friends who desperately want to hang on to their role as cowriters of your story. They will see the new you and listen to your ideas and feel the need to "talk you off the ledge" to keep you grounded. There will be days your writing style shifts from perhaps love story, where you love yourself and others unconditionally, into horror where you experience feelings of shame, guilt, or despair. Stop and troubleshoot! Embrace the new beliefs you have created. Remind yourself that you have a firm understanding of who you are and where you are going. Remind yourself of your purpose. Those are the tools you need to deal with all of this effectively. That's really all it takes. Remember, a belief is a recurring thought and nothing more than what happened in the past. You are *past* that now. Embrace the you that you are becoming.

Carve your name on hearts, not tombstones. A legacy is etched into the minds of others and the stories they share about you.

—SHANNON ALDER

Your Legacy

Often when people hear the word *legacy*, they think of money or the possessions people leave behind once they transition. Your legacy can be so much more. Long after you no longer have contact with a person, he or she will remember you. The question is: what do you want to be remembered for?

When you travel through life along your journey, your experiences, your story, will contribute to future generations. I want to be remembered as someone who lived an inspired life. Someone whose story helped to shape the stories of others as they find the courage to live their truth. This book will be part of my legacy, as it is filled with stories and lessons from my journey intended to inspire a world filled with love, joy, and kindness. It starts here, with you.

You, too, must decide what you want your legacy to be and begin building it now. Creating and living your BUS story is living the life you want to be remembered for. It is a life of service, knowledge, positivity, and inspiration. Your BUS story allows you to do the things that matter to you. When your day-to-day decisions are based on your legacy, you can spend your time and resources creating and living your BUS story. Your life will have meaning and purpose.

You will show up each day as if you are affecting the generations that come after you to leave their mark on the world. You will live your life as if you, and all who come after you, matter.

Wayne Dyer, the philosopher, author, and motivational speaker who I mentioned earlier in this chapter, chose to live an intentional life in which he shared his special gifts with others. His was the gift of motivation. He intuitively knew how to share enough of himself and his experiences to shape the minds of other people and to influence them to change their lives for the better. He lived and died doing what he loved. He wrote more than forty books and appeared on television and radio shows. He didn't keep his fire trapped within, and because of this, he left a legacy that continues to impact people, like me, across the globe years after his death.

> *I've learned that people will forget what you said, people will forget what you did, but people will never forget how you made them feel.*
>
> —MAYA ANGELOU

Whether it is your intention or not, you will be remembered not for what you did for people but for how you made them feel. When people are inspired by you and your special gifts, that is how you will be remembered. In chapter two, I told the story of the school custodian who made such an impact on students that the entire town turned out for her funeral. She wasn't a wealthy woman. She wasn't a CEO or the owner of a large corporation. She did what she did with love, and she shared her special gift with her students across multiple generations. She lived an intentional life. She mattered, and so do you.

What is your legacy? Are you living a life of intention? Are you accomplishing the things that matter most in your

The Beauty Underneath the Struggle

life, or are you putting them off for tomorrow or some day? Are you sharing your special gift with the world? You were created to affect lives. You were created for greatness. Everything you have experienced up until this point has influenced the trajectory of your life. Nothing you've gone through—both the good and the bad—will be lost. Your BUS story, whatever that may be, will give someone else hope. Your story will inspire others to live their dreams. Your pain and the lessons you have learned along the way will be used to heal someone else's pain and to teach someone else a lesson. Your joy will inspire someone else to keep going when they feel like giving up. Commit to living and leaving a legacy, and your life will never be the same again.

Commit to change now!

Go to Chapter 5: **BE** Grateful, *Your Legacy* in your workbook and complete the exercise.

6

BElieve

"There is a surrendering to your story and then a knowing that you don't have to stay in your story."

—COLETTE BARON-REID

Your Story

I grew up in a family where I wasn't valued or appreciated... This was the story I told myself for several years of my life.

When I was a young girl, I struggled with negative thinking, so much that I had convinced myself that I was a disappointment to my parents. This feeling of inadequacy seemed to magnify when I did things that let my parents down, and as a young girl, that was too often. I thought if I were smarter, prettier, or more pleasing, my parents would be prouder of me and would love me more. Of course, this

123

wasn't true, but since I chose to believe it, it became my truth.

As I got older and became more curious about my parents' stories, I learned that their stories were very similar to the one I had created. They both have expressed feelings of not being valued and appreciated. These same perceptions that they experienced growing up seemed to have extended into our family, manifesting in our relationships with one another.

It was not until several years later that I gained insight into what was happening. This cycle of not feeling valued and appreciated continued to present itself from one generation to the next. Why? Because we were unaware of the problem.

I recall a funny story I heard a while back that serves as a great example of how beliefs when left unquestioned will continue to move from one generation to the next. It goes something like this:

There was a favorite family recipe for a holiday ham that had been passed down from generation to generation. As the mother was preparing the ham for the umpteenth time, she was teaching her newly married daughter how to prepare the ham.

The mother delicately cut off both ends of the ham, placed it in the pan, and added the family's secret ingredients. Her daughter, who was watching, asked, "So why do you cut off the ends?"

Her mother answered, "Because that is how my mother taught me to do it." Later, the mother began to wonder why they cut off the ends, so she called her mother to ask.

The grandmother explained, "Because that is how my mother taught me to do it." The grandmother then wondered too, so she asked her elderly mother.

The great grandmother replied, "You don't need to cut off the ends! I always did that because my old oven was too small for a big pan."

This story holds a good lesson: our unexamined beliefs impact our decisions, and our decisions can impact our story for generations to come. Being mindful of our behaviors and ultimately our choices will help us notice and become more curious about our thoughts, feelings, and beliefs which will renew our family belief systems.

While the ham story is a funny, innocent example of how beliefs are passed on, other behaviors can be quite harmful when they go unquestioned. When these beliefs and behaviors are accepted as part of your belief system, we tend to project these feelings onto others or events throughout our life. This projection is then like a vicious cycle that doesn't end. Just like the daughter in the ham story, it is important that we begin to question where certain behaviors and beliefs originated so that we can make a conscious choice as to whether this pattern of thinking is serving us in a positive way or a negative way.

Once I changed my beliefs and began modeling new behaviors, the negative stories I had been telling myself slowly begin to change, and as a result, I could use the remaining pages to write more fulfilling stories while using my eraser to edit the stories that did not serve me well.

What stories are you telling yourself about your childhood or other experiences that are preventing you from moving on to the next chapter? What personal behaviors or beliefs can you begin to transform to get different results?

Using the Eraser to Edit Your Story

I am worthy!

My parents love me and support me in all that I want to accomplish...

"I am so proud of you," my mom said, as I read her excerpts from this book you're now holding. "That's going to be a best seller!"

"You have always been a special kid, and I am just so proud of the woman you've become," my Dad said during a two-hour phone conversation we had a few weeks ago.

Since I've learned the power of erasing and editing my story, questioning my thoughts, and finding new meaning

The Beauty Underneath the Struggle

in my previous narratives, I have gained new insight into my childhood perceptions, which now allow new experiences to flow onto the remaining pages of my life.

In the book *The Shadow Effect*, author Deepak Chopra tells us that "to avoid feeling that we're not good enough, we see others around us as not good enough...Everyone uses projection as a defense to avoid looking inward."[13] The template of projection is the following statement: "I can't admit what I feel, so I'll imagine that you feel it."[14] To break the cycle of projecting, the answer is not to reject the feeling, emotion, or belief but to wake up from it, admit it is happening, and own the feelings that you are projecting. Chopra says, "Until you make peace with negative feelings, they will persist."[15]

Once I began taking responsibility for what I was feeling, I began to challenge my negative beliefs about myself and started sharing more positive stories. I was able to address them, change them, and move from a horror story to new beginnings, slowly breaking the cycle of beliefs that had been handed down from generation to generation.

---

[13] Deepak Chopra, *The Shadow Effect* (New York: HarperCollins Publishers, 2009), 17.

[14] Chopra, *The Shadow Effect*, 17.

[15] Chopra, *The Shadow Effect*, 42.

Without our childhoods, without all our experiences, and without our time in family belief camp, we would not have evolved into the people we are today. My passion, wisdom, love, and determination are rooted in the experiences I had as a child. When you realize that there are no mistakes, you move into a place of peace and acceptance, knowing that everything is exactly as it should be. I am blessed and honored that I was chosen for this life so that I can share my gift with you.

Over the past few years my parents and I have grown emotionally closer and stronger together. I will often share with them what I've learned on my journey, which has inspired them to look within and confront some of their own beliefs and attitudes. My parents have been my top cheerleaders on this journey, lifting me up when I'm feeling down and encouraging me to move ahead. I am blessed that they are still here as I write these words.

Mom, Dad—I want you to know that you have encouraged and influenced me to be the woman I am today, and for this, I love you and appreciate you.

Using Your Power of Choice to Write Your Story

As you write your story and begin to move past the blockages we discussed earlier, you will need to remember a

The Beauty Underneath the Struggle

powerful weapon you have at your disposal every second of each day, and that is the power of *choice*. Until you realize that you choose your thoughts, your beliefs, and your behaviors, you will continue to be at the whim of everyone else's plan for your life. You are the one who must choose whether or not to hold the pencil; you are the one who gets to choose what to write.

When I decided to leave my school and start a new journey, I was a ball of emotions. I had set my feet upon a new path, and my journey as a principal was over. On my last day, when I placed the final box in my car to go home, I felt a sense of relief, but it was mixed with fear and uncertainty about the inevitable twists and turns of my new path. One thing I knew is that I wouldn't be able to create and develop a business out of fear. I had made a choice. I knew if I were going to be successful on my new journey, I would have to push through my fears and focus my attention on what I wanted to create. I had to be intentional about first believing it and then setting out to make it happen.

Like every new journey, it started with a choice. Life is a matter of choice. The ability to choose is not exclusive to me or to a set number of people; we all have the freedom to choose.

Barry Schwartz discusses the official dogma of all Western societies in his book *The Paradox of Choice*. He believes that to maximize the welfare of citizens is to maximize individual freedom. Freedom is good, worthwhile, and essential to being human. We maximize freedom by maximizing choice.[16] Life is a series of choices. We make millions of choices in our lifetimes and hundreds of choices each day: when to wake up, what to wear, what to eat, what we think about. It's all a choice. We can choose to make a series of steps to improve our lives, or we can sit on the sidelines and watch life pass us by. Creating and living your BUS story is a choice. Just as it is possible to choose to take the steps to create your BUS story, it is possible to choose not to.

> *"Your life changes the moment you make a new, congruent, and committed decision."*
>
> —TONY ROBBINS

The Choice Is Always Yours

"Make it a great day or not. The choice is yours." This is how my principal ended morning announcements each day when I served as a curriculum coordinator for an elementary school in North Carolina. At the time, it made no sense to me why she would say, "The choice is yours."

---

[16] Barry Schwartz, *The Paradox of Choice* (New York: HarperCollins Publishers, 2016).

How could we possibly determine whether our day was going to be good or bad? How could we control the events of the day?

It took me a few years to understand and embrace this message of choice fully. During my time at Piney Grove Elementary, listening to this message almost every morning, I never understood what it meant or how to apply it. It wasn't until I became a principal that I began to feel and understand the magnitude of this statement. Here I was in a leadership position, trying to motivate, encourage, and inspire my team members to bring their "A" game to work each day, and I never realized that it would have to be their choice, not mine, to bring their personal best. I could set the conditions so that they would want to bring their "A" game, but I learned that ultimately the choice would be theirs. Leaders cannot be responsible for others' behavior, but they can hold them accountable when behaviors do not align with the team's mission and agreements. How we show up each day is like choosing an outfit to wear; it's all a choice.

Discovering your BUS story will begin with making different choices. But first, you will need to understand how your past choices have influenced your current reality. Many of the choices we make, when practiced repeatedly, form habits. And habits are challenging to change.

When we are unable to conceptualize the infinite possibilities or choices in any given situation, we become stagnant, unable to move, or unable to embrace new decisions. We may begin to believe that everything is happening to us rather than accepting we have some control over our lives. We repeat the same routines, such as going to work, coming home, watching television, and going to bed, never realizing that these are all choices we've made. We blame our jobs, our bosses, our spouses, and sometimes our children when we're not able to do the things we've longed to do. If only we realized that the choice is ours.

Nothing Different Will Happen in Your Life Unless You're Willing to Do Something Different!

As young children, we rely on the adult figures in our lives, such as our parents, teachers, aunts, and even pastors to provide us with guidance or to make choices for us. We sometimes become so reliant on this support and direction that we fail to consider the things we desire, and we can grow up feeling the need for approval from our friends, bosses, coworkers, or others in our lives. We believe that our happiness is dependent upon others being happy with our choices.

We attend the college our parents want us to attend, we marry the guy because he wants to get married, and we have another baby because everyone else says it's time. We begin to feel like we're living inside someone else's story and not creating our own. When we do what others want us to do and not what we desire, it can be emotionally oppressive and eventually cause us to become unhappy, frustrated, or even angry.

The choices we make (or do not make) begin to form a pattern of behavior that may serve us well as children, but as we grow physically, mentally, and spiritually, some of these choices can limit us. Accepting a belief that our choices are limited or, even worse, that we don't have a choice, will keep us from reaching for those things we really want. The key is to understand that in any given situation, we have the right to choose. Remember, nothing different will happen in your life if you're not willing to do something different. This can be challenging because at times our choices operate on the subconscious level, the part of our brain where things happen automatically. When you make the same choices repeatedly, it may feel like your choices are not your own.

Whenever I was working in a job and started to feel like things had become too routine, I would take a day off as a reminder to myself that going to work was my choice. You will have to do something different to realize that it is a choice. It's your choice to stay in an unhealthy relationship, it's your choice to remain at a job that makes you miserable, it's your choice to host your family for the holidays—all of these things are choices, and guess what? The choice is yours.

"You've got to take action before the emotion passes."
—JIM ROHN

If you are committed to change and creating and living your BUS story, examining your choices is essential. Many times, you will get these brilliant ideas only to talk yourself out them. When an idea enters your mind that is going to propel you or help someone else, act on it before you talk yourself out of it. I say this because many times our creativity will wake us up and enter our minds and say things like: apply for the job, ask her out, or make the phone call. At the time of the thought's conception, there is a lot of energy surrounding the idea to make it happen. But the slower you respond, the more likely the energy will subside, and you will probably end up not doing it at all!

The other morning at three o'clock, the universe gave me the title of my second Baelor Book, a series of children's books I'm writing to help kids develop a healthy mindset. "Kindness is contagious too!" the voice said. I got up out of bed and immediately began to write the story. It's a fascinating story that teaches kids that kindness, like a virus, is contagious too! I wrote the story in about three hours, and I'm proud to say that I just sent it to my illustrators yesterday!

Check Yourself Before You Wreck Yourself

Commit to asking yourself self-check questions when you feel your choices are limited; this will help you to transform your belief system so that you can weigh the alternatives.

1. **S versus S.** Is this choice serving me or stopping me?
2. **Mine versus Theirs.** Does this choice belong to me, or does it belong to my parents, siblings, friends, et cetera?
3. **Never say never.** Can I find one other person who has been successful doing this?

Let's take a closer look at these questions and pair them with examples. Let's say you have had a long-standing desire to open a cafe serving people in your community. You are passionate about the vision, you've done the research, and you know in your gut that your business would be a great contribution to the community. However, you notice that every time you get closer to moving forward on signing the lease on that new building, thoughts of failure invade your mind. You begin to make excuses, and you decide to cancel the appointment. To tackle this issue, you can go through the self-check questions above. Is this choice serving me or stopping me? Well, you have canceled the appointment to sign the lease multiple times, so the choice is certainly stopping you from pursuing your dream. Next question. Does the belief that I will fail belong to me or someone else I know? You think back to all the times your dad told you never to start a business and all the arguments he and your mom had about his own failing business. In this example, you realize that your dad's advice to you is influencing your choice to start your own business. So the advice your dad gave you belonged to him, not you. And finally, you ask yourself if someone else has been successful making this choice. You may think to yourself, I'm hesitant because I have seen the negative experiences my dad went through; however, are there successful business owners in my community? The answer, of course, will be yes. If you have seen it in someone else, you know the same can be true for you. Say it aloud.

Your turn! Go to Chapter 6: BElieve in your workbook and put the self-check questions into practice!

Love Your Story

Like many of us, I wear several hats—wife, mother, grand-mother, business owner, motivational speaker, and so many more. In the quest to create and live my BUS story, I have experienced joy and pain, failure and achievement, and fear and courage. These highs and lows aren't exclusive to me and my story: we all experience them. Life isn't linear; we don't go from point A to point B without the twists or turns that being human throws our way. Sometimes we may feel like we are soaring in certain areas of our lives, whether it be finances, health, or relationships, while simultaneously struggling in other areas, like work, education, or parent-hood. The highs and lows are all a part of the journey. You see, there would be no light if darkness had never existed: it takes having a life of both bliss and struggle to create the beauty we all seek in life.

When I go out and speak, I encourage my audiences first to understand that they are the creators of their sto-ries. To change anything, you first must believe and accept your ability to choose a response. I remind them that you decided to become an educator or to work in this position; and just like you made a choice to accept this position, you can make a choice to do something different. I cannot tell you the number of times people have asked me what I do. And when I reveal to them that I'm an educator, their response is usually something like, "Bless your heart," or "Oh, I feel so sorry for you, and all you have to go through." These types of responses will sometimes make educators feel sorry for themselves. We start to adopt a feeling of victimhood. So I must remind my fellow educators to wake up: you are not a victim; you are a victor!

These feelings of self-pity are among the reasons we come to work angry, overwhelmed, and frustrated. We forget that we don't "*have to*" be in this position, we forget our power to choose. Taking responsibility for our attitudes may sound like an easy thing to do, but it's not. We have become accustomed to placing the blame on something or someone for the things in our lives that we don't like. Taking ownership allows us to hold the pencil and become conscious of our ability to make choices. This will help us to put our pencil to paper to write the story we desire.

When you learn to love your story, you understand that every part of your story is important. You live with no regrets, as you now understand that every experience was designed to help create the person that you are today. You and your story are enough. We can be tough on ourselves, resorting to negative self-talk about our past choices. Are you still replaying scenes from mistakes you made and reanalyzing the choices you have made in the past? Often when we are on the path to create better stories for ourselves, we beat ourselves up when we make a mistake or if we're not achieving our goals as quickly and smoothly as we initially thought we would. Maybe you "cheated" on your diet plan. Maybe you didn't get the job you applied for. Maybe you are experiencing a lull in your business. Instead of beating yourself up with feelings of unworthiness, accept things as they come and continue pushing forward. From the moment we wake up, we are bombarded with responsibility; we have our family, work, health, and many other things to care for. Give yourself permission to love yourself and focus on the things that are important to you. Loving you. Loving your story. There is no higher calling than that.

Won't He Do It!

I had the pleasure of interviewing Mr. Cleveland Mouton, or "Mouton," as I lovingly refer to him, one of the teachers I hired during my time as a principal in Texas. Mouton was one of the most dynamic, innovative, energetic educators I had ever met!

I first met Mouton at a job fair our district was hosting in April 2015, and from the moment we met, I was in love with his charisma, energy, and positivity! When Mouton pulled out his phone to share a video that he had created with his students, I was sold! I knew that students in our school would benefit from his teaching style! And boy, was I right! Students, teachers, and families loved Mr. Mouton!

Mouton shared with me that when he attended the job fair back in April 2015, he was not interested in moving to Texas. He had agreed to ride with a friend who wanted to attend the job fair and later convinced him to participate. Mr. Mouton ended up buying an outfit to wear and printing several copies of his résumé.

At the time all of this was happening, he had recently learned that he had not been selected for an assistant principal position in his current district for which he had interviewed. Mouton says that he was really hurt (his struggle) because he thought he had the job.

Since elementary school, Mouton had been a goal setter; he would put his mind on something and would be determined to make it happen! In third grade, he had set a goal to become a teacher, and by sixth grade, he knew he wanted to become a principal. He was inspired by two people who had been instrumental in helping him through struggles: his third-grade teacher, Ms. Chong, and Mr. McCray, his elementary school principal.

Mouton ended up moving to Texas from Louisiana and accepted a third-grade math teacher position at the school where I was principal. In that same year, his first year

The Beauty Underneath the Struggle

teaching on our campus, he was named Campus Teacher of the Year (TOY)!

Mouton recalls coming into my office after being named TOY. He says I asked if he was going to apply for District Teacher of the Year. He then told me that he was working on it but felt he wouldn't win because this was his first year with the district. Mouton says that I told him, "Oh yes, you're going to win!" He states that I took a sticky note and wrote down, "Mouton will be District Teacher of the Year," and placed it on a vision board that hung in my office.

He ended up submitting his application after several revisions. And in April 2016, Mouton was named District Teacher of the Year for Fort Bend ISD, the eighth largest district in Texas.

Since that time, Mouton has accomplished many other goals, including becoming a principal of an elementary school in 2017. It's important to note that when Mouton came to our school/district, he came partly because he was disappointed because he was not selected for an assistant principal position with his district in Louisiana. But get this: Mouton skipped the assistant principal role altogether and was named principal of a school by 2017! Won't he do it? Napoleon Hill, an American self-help author, known best for his book *Think and Grow Rich*, says, "Whatever the mind can conceive and believe, the mind can achieve." Mr. Mouton serves as a witness to this truth.

Mr. Mouton

"To fall in love with yourself is the first secret to happiness."
—Robert Morley

Mouton says that he loves to share the story of his time in Texas with others to inspire them to believe in their dreams. When you love your story, you will be better prepared to love and serve others. Moving from a horror story to a love story in an authentic way is an act of service not only for yourself, but also for others around you. Your family, friends, and co-workers have a need for the inspiration you provide through living and loving your story. I want to encourage you to shake things up a bit! Take risks even if the current story is working for you because nothing more will happen if you continue to make the same choices. If you're living, there are always goals to set, pursue, and achieve. There is always a higher level of consciousness waiting on the other side of choice.

Being intentional about your choices and taking risks will help you to create your best BUS story.

Each day I wake up with my pencil in hand, I am filled with purpose, joy, and fulfillment—loving the story and life I get to create.

Create your story, love your story, share it, and beat the drum for others brave enough to share their stories with the world.

Struggles Need Love Too!

As I reflect on my story, I love every part of the journey—getting married, having children, going from being a classroom assistant in a school to becoming a principal. The road to pursuing my dream of motivating leaders, teachers, and students at one school to now hundreds of schools across the country. Your story is more than the outcome; it's making the conscious decision to be present in the moment and loving the process as it unfolds. That doesn't mean just loving the parts that feel good, the parts that work. Love it all! Love the hardships, the struggles, the times you get knocked down. Love it because they are not failures; they are lessons that give you more of what you need to continue writing. Your story is yours to love and cherish.

Live your passion. Live your dreams. Remember your mission statement. Do not let the fear of risk hold you back. You have gifts. You have a story to share. You have a story to love because it's uniquely your own. At the end of life, when you reflect on all that you were able to accomplish, regret will not be part of your legacy, because you have chosen to create and live your BUS story. You chose to use your story and gifts to inspire others. You chose to create a vision and use that vision to propel your life forward. Make it a good life or not; the choice is yours.

Commit to change now!

7

BE Awesome

What Is Your Writing Style Now?

Congratulations. You now have the tools to create your BUS story! Before I let you go, let's take some time to look at your progress so far by assessing your writing style. This will provide you with more clarity and direction as you take a good look at yourself and your accomplishments. There will always be something to celebrate, and now is your opportunity!

Knowing your writing style will help you to stay focused when you have a difficult time conceptualizing your dreams. My dream was to become a singer and ultimately to reach people on a larger scale. Though I didn't become a singer, I now use my voice to bring joy and inspiration to audiences all over the country. You can only live your BUS story when you identify and are honest about where you are now and create a clear vision of where you want to be.

When you identify your writing style, not only will this improve your life, but you will also become a gift as your actions impact the entire world.

"The most creative act you will ever undertake is the act of creating yourself."

—DEEPAK CHOPRA

In chapter two, you were introduced to the five types of writing styles, which can help you to determine where your energy resides most often. Let's take some time to assess your writing style once more. With the ups and downs of life, twists and turns, it can be difficult to pinpoint just one writing style; plus we move in and out of these styles all the time. The most important thing is to be open and vulnerable so that your true style is revealed to you. Let's review the writing styles chart once more below.

The Beauty Underneath the Struggle

Writer's Style Chart
Where are you right now?

The chart below describes five types of writers. In a lifetime, you will move in and out of these levels. The goal is to notice where you reside most often as you choose where you want to be.

Love Story

This writer believes that love is unchanging. A love for self and others is unconditional. This person believes that we are better together. He knows that if one person wins, we all win. The sole purpose of his story is to inspire others to tell theirs.

Comedy

This writer sees life as enjoyable, unattached to outcomes. He doesn't take himself, people, or events that happen in his story personally. He sees life as a big opportunity to make a difference.

Rebirth/Awakening

This writer realizes that *he* is the author of his story. He is no longer blaming and complaining, but feeling empowered to take 100 percent responsibility for his story (his decisions, actions, behaviors, and results).

Drama/Action

This writer is driven by conflict and has a strong identification to the ego. This writer believes that the world should conform to him. His anger/frustration will often move him beyond the victim (no action) to being fueled to take action.

Horror

This writer is tied up into emotional energy of shame, guilt, fear, and despair, which ultimately makes him the victim of his story. This type of writer is not the writer at all as he allows others (and events) to dictate how his story should go.

© Niki Spears 2020

Remember, the goal is to notice where you reside most often and where you strive to be. Begin by asking yourself questions. Start with the overarching question: What type of writer am I now? Explore the type of writer you are by first being honest with yourself. Schedule some time alone and go within and evaluate your thoughts and feelings about events and experiences that have occured in your life. Once you identify your feelings regarding these events, write them down. Here are some examples of questions you can use to help you determine your writing style.

- If I had to describe my life with five words, how would I describe it?
- When was I the happiest with my life?
- Which experiences would I like to have more of?
- What has been the most frustrating thing in my life?
- If I had to list three things that went well in the past year, what would they be?
- If I had to list three things that went poorly in the past year, what would they be?
- What lessons have I learned in the past five years?
- How do I fill voids in my life?

As you ask yourself these questions, write down the first

thing that comes to mind without overanalyzing. When you have completed writing, you will notice patterns. Take it all in and appreciate it all.

Now refer back to the writing styles chart, paying close attention to feelings and emotions that describe where you are or where you reside most often. Do not be discouraged if you have identified a style that brings low-level energy, as this does not mean it defines *who* you are, only *where* your emotional energy is. Allow the feelings to flow in so that you can determine their source, accept them, and take action to do something about them. When you learn to love yourself unconditionally, you will feel the power of gratitude at work in your life. You realize the sole purpose of your story is to inspire others to tell theirs. My hope is that you take what you have learned from this experience and take action.

Which writing style do you find yourself engaged in most often? Turn to Chapter 7: **BE** Awesome, *What Is Your Writing Style Now?*

Owning Your Awesomeness

Nothing about you is an accident; everything about you was created for a reason. When you hide your awesomeness from others, you are doing a disservice not only to yourself but also to others around you. Imagine for a moment that you are a gorgeous fish swimming around in a dark ocean. The ocean has been dark for several years, and no one has yet determined how to bring light. You are afraid to show others your beautiful, bright colors that glow in the dark, so you cover them with mud so you will not stand out among the others. This goes on for several years, until one day, there is a huge wave that sweeps the ocean floor. The current is so strong that it washes away the mud and reveals your glowing fins. All of a sudden, the ocean opens up, and you are surrounded by the brightest light you have ever seen. Your light is so bright that you now notice that the same fish you have been swimming with for several years are also unique in color. When you allow your light to shine, you open up dark waters for others to shine through.

When you create your BUS story, you will need to allow your light to shine. This light is your special gift to the world; it's your awesomeness. We all have it, but often, like the fish who covered himself with mud, we keep it hidden deep inside ourselves. Your awesomeness is meant to be shared!

Everything we are—good and even what we consider bad—is all a part of our awesomeness. Our divine gift should radiate from us and be shared with the world.

We all have the potential for greatness, not just when things are going well, but also in moments of struggle. What you have, what you know, and who you are, are meant to fill a specific need. Someone in this world needs what you have to offer, so resist the urge to hide your awesomeness. Don't diminish yourself or your talents just to make others feel better. Like the fish, when you share your gifts and talents with others, you are inherently giving them permission to share theirs.

You must decide if you are going to rob the world or bless it with the rich, valuable, potent, untapped resources locked away within you.

—MYLES MUNROE

What would you attempt if you couldn't fail? If you had the chance to improve this world, what would you do?

As you prepare to write your BUS story, here are some reminders to take with you on your journey:

1. **Align your life with your passions**. Listen to your heart as well as your desires. What could you lose yourself in for hours, creating or recreating? When you look around, what calls out to you for you to improve with your special touch? What would you be doing if you didn't consider money, family, or other obligations? That's your calling!

2. **Acknowledge your special gifts**. Take care to sharpen your special gifts and share them with the world. It is not fair to you or the rest of the world when you shrink yourself and hide your gifts.

3. **Declare.** Decide right now to live an intentional life. You have created a mission statement. Read that mission statement before bed each night and first thing in the morning to set the tone for your day. Do as I did on the treadmill that morning in March 2016, and actually imagine yourself doing what you love. Paint a clear picture in your mind of what that is and take the steps to do it. Everything starts in the mind!

4. **Believe in yourself**. You write your own story; believe in your power as the creator of your life. We all have the tendency to doubt ourselves by considering our failures when attempting something new or challenging; resist the urge to do that. Think of all the things you have accomplished that were once difficult, but that require little thought to complete now. That could be as simple as riding a bike, cooking a simple meal, or driving a car. The point is that at one time, it was a struggle, and you thought you would never master it, but now it is second nature.

5. **Protect yourself from low-level conversations**. When you have a big enough goal, someone in your

The Beauty Underneath the Struggle

life will feel the urge to warn you, to keep you in the safe bubble that he or she has created. Ignore the limiting beliefs; they do not belong to you.

6. **Be brave**. Do that one thing you don't think you can do. Comfort zones are created from limiting beliefs. When you are willing to step outside of your comfort zone is when the magic happens. And finally...

7. **Expect to be great**. There will be times when it feels like nothing you are working toward is showing up in your life. Expect greatness to happen at any moment. Adopt a mantra for yourself. Mine is: "I am protected by divine wisdom and guidance. I cannot fail. I am destined for greatness!"

When you believe you are wired for greatness, the universe will conspire to ensure that you are surrounded by great things. Sustained focus with positive energy will cause your vision to come to life. Greatness is within you.

Now it is time for you to write, edit, and share your BUS story as you inspire others to find the beauty underneath the struggle.

Commit to change now!

8

BE Free to BE YOU!
Your BUS Story!

Your turn!

These next few pages have been reserved for you to write one of your best BUS stories. Remember, throughout the course of your journey, you will have several opportunities to create a BUS story. It starts here with you as you learn to embrace the beauty underneath the struggle.

Commit to change now!

Turn to Chapter 8: **BE** Free to **BE** YOU! Write Your BEST BUS Story!

THE **B**EAUTY **U**NDERNEATH THE **S**TRUGGLE

CREATING

YOUR BUS STORY

WORKBOOK

NIKI SPEARS

CREATING YOUR BUS STORY — THE **B**EAUTY **U**NDERNEATH THE **S**TRUGGLE

8 B's to Create Your BUS Story

1) BE Responsible ~100%

2) BE Aware

3) BE Open

4) BE Courageous

5) BE Grateful

6) BElieve

7) BE Awesome

8) BE Free to **BE** You! Your BUS Story!

Workbook Exercises

Writing Your BUS Story Journal Exercises

Chapter 1: BE Responsible!

The Power of Taking 100 Percent Responsibility for Your Story
What events/circumstances are you refusing to own?

Using the chart below, think of situations in your life that you are unhappy with right now—this could be your marriage, your job, or even your current state of mind. Once you've identified some of these things, think about whom you've given power over these circumstances; in other words, whom do you hold responsible?

If others, like your parents, siblings, bosses, teachers, friends, come to mind—mark through them and place the word *me* in all caps! ME stands for "my energy." It is your energy, and you can use this energy first to take ownership and then to take action to tell yourself a different story (if it is from the past), or take action to do something about it (if it is something current). Write down what you will do/ say to move forward from these situations.

Remember, you don't have the power to change the behaviors of others, but you do possess the power to change yourself.

What things in your life are you unhappy with?	Who is responsible?	What are you willing to do/say to move forward?

Congratulations! By taking responsibility for your story, you will have the opportunity to take your pencil and do more than simply write; you can now plan, design, and create your masterpiece. When you are the one holding the pencil, you can make sure things happen for you, and not just to you.

Chapter 2: BE Aware
Identifying Core Beliefs—Follow the Why!

Welcome back! Now let's spend some time reflecting on some of your beliefs by jotting them down in the space

The Beauty Underneath the Struggle

below. This could be as simple as "I am shy," "I am smart," or "the world is a cruel place." Whatever those thoughts are that pop into your head most often, and you have adopted as part of your belief system, jot them down now. During this part, we will use the honor system. Remember, this entire experience belongs to you. For you to move from where you are, you must be honest about what is happening in your mind. We assure you that we won't share your thoughts with anyone. Oh, if you need more space, please use a composition notebook to accompany the work you will do during your workbook exercises.

Some of my beliefs about myself, others, and the world are:

Now, pick one of the core beliefs you have identified and scroll down to the source. Remember, beliefs are not always negative; it's also important to understand where your positive beliefs originated so that you can begin inviting more positive experiences in your life.

Start by picking a thought that is constant or recurrent in your mind and follow the thread of that thought, all the way down until you find the time when it was first posted on your time line. Ask yourself, "Why do I feel this way?" Like a detective, continue to ask yourself why until you get closer to the root of the belief. There is a reason behind every response. Follow it all the way back until you understand your beliefs enough to navigate them. Follow the why.

Belief	Why?	Why?	Why?
If I don't work hard, I will fail and not be able to financially support myself and my family.	You must work hard to succeed.	If you don't work hard, you will have to rely on others.	I fear having to rely on others to support me. Why? As a young girl, when my parents would have disagreements, I would hear my dad say that everything belonged to him—the money, cars, even the house we lived in. Although his words were not directed at me, I often felt insecure and unworthy. My New Story: I am worthy!
Belief	Why?	Why?	Why? Why? New Story:

The Positive Thinking Model

Niki Spears, 2019

Looking at the model, think about the thousands of thoughts our mind is bombarded with each day; the first phase shows that these thoughts reside outside our mind until we make a choice to move to the second phase of accepting these thoughts as true. This is when they enter not only our minds but also our spirits. Once we adopt or accept the beliefs, they move into the third phase, which is experiencing the feeling or emotion attached to the thoughts. Finally, once we move to the fourth phase, we have accepted these beliefs as our truth, and our behavior will cause us to react or respond to the emotions that come with the new or recurring beliefs.

For example, you may have a thought that your boss doesn't like you. If you accept that your boss doesn't like you, this now becomes your belief. This may cause you to feel unappreciated, which may result in you consistently calling in sick and ultimately looking for another job. What do you think would happen if you had not accepted this thought? What would be some possible behavioral outcomes?

When you look between each phase of the thinking model, there is one thing that stands out and that is the power to choose. This means that no matter where you are in the process, it is never too late to choose differently.

Discovering Your Gifts

Now it's your turn! Using the next chart, take a few moments to reflect on these questions:

Name your special talents (things that seem effortless and you're really good at doing).	
What brings a smile to your face? (Look at the list above: which ones bring you the most joy when you're engaged in them?)	
If there was no concern about pay, what would you be doing?	

The Beauty Underneath the Struggle

Use this information to write your purpose statement:
I exist to:

What are the goals you would like to achieve?
Write down your goals in the space below and the actions you will take to achieve them. If there is a person you will trust to hold you accountable (include yourself here as well, as ultimately it will be your responsibility to ensure you follow your plan), write his or her name in the space indicated. Your goals will serve as your table of contents as you develop your BUS story.

Goal	Steps to achieve that goal	Accountability partner
Example: Be more active	Exercise three days a week. Ride a bike every Saturday.	Me

Chapter 3: BE Open

Think of a negative story you've been telling yourself about a person or an event. For example, you could think, "I'll never get promoted" or "I'll never find the right guy/girl." Whatever the negative story is, write it down in the following space:

Negative Version of the Story:

Read the negative story once more. Now, consider a more encouraging account of the story—a more positive reason something happened or did not happen.

Positive Version of the Story:

Now read the positive version of the story again. How does it make you feel?

Your story is a conscious reminder to be, to exist, to live exactly the way that pleases you—in the way you enjoy. When you are continually telling yourself negative stories about your abilities, your childhood, or the events that happen in your life, this can bring on writer's block, preventing you from moving forward and writing the next chapters of your life. Now let's return to the book and discuss negative self-talk.

Chapter 4: BE Courageous
Transforming What If Stories...

Think of a risk(s) you've been tempted to take, but you have created the worst-case scenario in your head, which prevented you from taking the risk altogether. Below, create "what if things go right" stories that allow you to create more positive outcomes. While you are creating your "what if something goes right" stories, consider the actions you'll need to take to make these stories a reality.

What if this goes right...	What actions will I need to take to make this true?
Example: I get the promotion!	Study for my interview, consult the right people regarding my current strengths/ opportunities, have a positive attitude.

Surround Yourself with Positive People

Assess the characters in your story. Think of the people who are currently in your life. Determine whether they are adding positive energy to your story to propel you forward or constantly bringing negative energy.

Name of character (person)	Relationship to you	Brings positive energy (PE) or negative energy (NE)	Evidence
Kermit	Husband	PE	Supports me in my endeavors, loves me unconditionally, takes care of me, sees the greatness in everything I do.

If most of the people in your story are bringing you negative energy, you will need to reflect on your own energy to determine the frequency you are sending out to the world.

Chapter 5: BE Grateful
The Power of Gratitude

The power of keeping a gratitude journal cannot be

The Beauty Underneath the Struggle

overestimated. When we turn our focus from the things we don't have to the things we do, our energy is transformed, and more joy enters our minds and spirits.

I want to encourage you to pick out a notebook, tablet, or composition book and begin your gratitude journal today. It can be as simple as including the date, the day of the week, and a list of all the things that bring you joy in that moment.

Let's try it now!

Today I am grateful for...

_____

_____

_____

_____

Your Legacy

If you live a life of purpose, how will you be remembered? Write it:

Draw it:

Chapter 6: BElieve

Think of a decision you need to make about something now or in the near future. Commit to asking yourself the self-check questions if you feel your choices are limited. This will help you to transform your belief system so that you can weigh the alternatives.

Describe the Decision:
1. S versus S. Is this choice serving me or stopping me?

2. Mine versus Theirs. Does this choice belong to me, or does it belong to my parents, siblings, friends, et cetera?

3. Never say never. Can I find one other person who has successfully done this?

The Beauty Underneath the Struggle

Chapter 7: BE Awesome

Exercise: What Is Your Writing Style Now

Begin by reflecting. Start with the overarching question: What type of writer are you now? Explore the type of writer you are by first being honest with yourself. Schedule some time alone and think. Go within and evaluate events and experiences in your life. Once you are comfortable with your space, thoughts, and feelings, take out a pencil and write. Here are some examples of questions you can use to help you determine your writing style:

- If I had to describe my life with five words, how would I describe it?
- When was I the happiest with my life?
- Which experiences would I like to have more of?
- What has been the most frustrating thing in my life?
- If I had to list three things that went well in the past year, what would they be?
- If I had to list three things that went poorly in the past year, what would they be?
- What lessons have I learned in the past five years?
- How do I fill voids in my life?

Now look at the chart below and determine where your level of energy resides most often. Remember, this chart is fluid, and you will move in and out of these levels. The goal is to understand where you are so that you can make intentional actions to move where you would like to be.

The Beauty Underneath the Struggle

Writer's Style Chart
Where are you right now?

The chart below describes five types of writers. In a lifetime, you will move in and out of these levels. The goal is to notice where you reside most often as you choose where you want to be.

Love Story
This writer believes that love is unchanging. A love for self and others is unconditional. This person believes that we are better together. He knows that if one person wins, we all win. The sole purpose of his story is to inspire others to tell theirs.

Comedy
This writer sees life as enjoyable, unattached to outcomes. He doesn't take himself, people, or events that happen in his story personally. He sees life as a big opportunity to make a difference.

Rebirth/Awakening
This writer realizes that *he* is the author of his story. He is no longer blaming and complaining, but feeling empowered to take 100 percent responsibility for his story (his decisions, actions, behaviors, and results).

Drama/Action
This writer is driven by conflict and has a strong identification to the ego. This writer believes that the world should conform to him. His anger/frustration will often move him beyond the victim (no action) to being fueled to take action.

Horror
This writer is tied up into emotional energy of shame, guilt, fear, and despair, which ultimately makes him the victim of his story. This type of writer is not the writer at all as he allows others (and events) to dictate how his story should go.

© Niki Spears 2020

Chapter 8: BE FREE to BE You! Your BUS Story!

These next few pages have been reserved for you to write one of your best BUS stories. Remember, throughout your journey, you will have several opportunities to create a BUS story. It starts here with you as you learn to embrace the beauty underneath the struggle.

The Beauty Underneath the Struggle

My Bus Story

Use the space below to write your special BUS Story.

Acknowledgments

I would like to express the highest gratitude to my husband, Kermit, who has supported me on this journey, always pushing me to believe that things could be "greater later." To my amazing parents, who are my cheerleaders. To my three daughters, who were so self-sufficient, allowing me to do what God called me to do without guilt or reservations. To my beautiful Aunt Francis, who has encouraged me since I was a little girl to write and share my story; to all my other aunts and uncles (those who are here in the physical and in spirit), who always made me feel *special*. To my sisters and brother for backing me no matter what! A special thanks to Donna Fontenot, who was sent to me by God to support me in my vision of creating Energy Bus for Schools and to the rest of my Energy Bus family currently on this journey, who believes and supports this vision of creating positive schools. To Veronica Sopher, who has been my rock through this entire book writing process. To all those who shared their struggles as part of this story—Keshun Brown, Latissue Colbert, Cleveland Mouton, Julie Ward Nee, and Shaughn Thomas. Your story is now our story.

I would also like recognize those that gave me amazing opportunities to expand my story and do the things that I was called to do: Ms. Kathy Carter, my principal at Brentwood Elementary, who hired me as a kindergarten teacher and recommended me for the University of Texas Principal Program; Nelson Coulter, my professor at University of Texas and one of the classroom observers, who after observing my classroom not once, but twice, recommended me for the principalship program, and someone who recognized my struggles as amazing opportunities; Guadalupe Velasquez, who gave me the opportunity to become an assistant principal with absolutely no prior experience; Sandy Sikes, my principal when I worked as a curriculum coordinator at Piney Grove Elementary in North Carolina, who hired me despite the district's recommendation to hire someone who had taught in the district; Charles Dupre, the first superintendent who recognized my gifts and afforded me several opportunities to work with him to impact schools/districts; Jon Gordon, author of *The Energy Bus*, who knew nothing about me but was obedient to God and allowed me to use his book to create opportunities for schools to create and sustain positive culture. And last but certainly not least, to all our Energy Bus Schools, who welcomed my team to become part of their story.

Bibliography

Canfield, Jack, and Janet Switzer. *The Success Principles: How to Get from Where You Are to Where You Want to Be*. New York: HarperCollins, 2005.

Chopra, Deepak, Debbie Ford, and Marianne Williamson. *The Shadow Effect: Illuminating the Hidden Power of Your True Self*. New York: HarperOne, 2009.

Dyer, Wayne W. *The Power of Intention*. Carlsbad: Hay House, 2004.

Goodreads. "God is Life in Action." Accessed April 1, 2020. https://www.goodreads.com/quotes/97787-god-is-life-god-is-life-in-action-the-best.

Hawkins, David R. *Power vs. Force: The Hidden Determinants of Human Behavior*. Carlsbad: Hay House, 2012.

King, Martin Luther, Jr. *Stride toward Freedom*. Boston: Beacon Press, 2010.

Manalo, Emmanuel, and Manu Kapur. "The Role of Failure in Promoting Thinking Skills and Creativity: New Findings and Insights about How Failure Can Be

Beneficial for Learning." *Thinking Skills and Creativity* 30 (2018). https://doi.org/10.1016/j.tsc.2018.06.001.

Schwartz, Barry. *The Paradox of Choice*. New York: HarperCollins Publishers, 2016.

Smith, Will. "Fault vs Responsibility." WhateverItTakesMotivation. Posted on January 31, 2018. YouTube video, 2:29. https://www.youtube.com/watch?v=USsqkd-E9ag.

Traugott, John. "Achieving Your Goals: An Evidence-Based Approach." Michigan State University. Last modified August 26, 2014. https://www.canr.msu.edu/news/achieving_your_goals_an_evidence_based_approach.

Author Biography

Niki Spears is a motivational speaker and author who has worked in education for more than twenty years. As a child Niki struggled with negative thinking about herself and the world, and as an adult began to embrace practices that would help her transform the negative self-talk into stories of opportunity. Niki now travels the United States encouraging educators to focus on their strengths and how they can use these talents to add value to the world. Niki lives in Houston, Texas, with her husband, three beautiful daughters, and one granddaughter, for whom her series of children's books, Baelor Books, are named.

Made in the USA
Las Vegas, NV
04 February 2021